Vancouver's Vengeance

A Novel
Barry Deane Stewart

As with *Drake's* Dilemma, this book is dedicated to everyone who loves history and what it teaches us, especially to those who are willing to challenge the conventional versions of events and to consider new alternatives. I hope that characteristic will be part of my grandchildren's legacy.

Order this book online at www.trafford.com
or email orders@trafford.com

Most Trafford titles are also available at major online book retailers.

Printed in the United States of America.

ISBN: 978-1-4907-0531-6 (sc)
ISBN: 978-1-4907-0532-3 (hc)
ISBN: 978-1-4907-0533-0 (e)

Library of Congress Control Number: 2013911085

Trafford rev. 08/24/2013

www.trafford.com

North America & international
toll-free: 1 888 232 4444 (USA & Canada)
fax: 812 355 4082

READER ALERT

This novel is a sequel to *Drake's Dilemma* by the same author. It is not necessary to read that book in order to get the full appreciation of the story in *Vancouver's Vengeance*. However, reading this story first will preclude much of the drama, uncertainty, and somewhat surprising ending to that earlier work.

Reactions to *Drake's Dilemma* and *Vancouver's Vengeance* by expert antiquarian book dealers and collectors:

"These novels capture the inner workings of the antiquarian book business exceptionally well."

"The author certainly knows the book collecting world very well. All of those wheeling-and-dealing events really happen."

"A serious book collector should definitely read these books to better understand the reality of dealing with international book sellers."

"Even rare-book sellers can learn something about their business here."

. . . and by readers:

"The author has given us a compelling story, a slice of history, and an excellent depiction of the antiquarian book world, all in one very readable novel."

"Sir Francis Drake and Captain George Vancouver become real people, with real personalities and real-life problems."

"What an easy way to learn about the exciting history of the early exploration of northwestern America. Who knew?"

"If we had history books like this in high school I would have paid a lot more attention."

"The stories are a great blending of historical events with the dynamics of modern rare-book collecting."

Reviews for *Across the Land*
. . . a Canadian journey of discovery

"(The book is) an uncritical upbeat trip from sea to sea to sea."

"(It's) contagious. Not far into the book, the reader is tempted to pack a bag, get in the car, and go find the Canada that Stewart sees."

"He mixes well-known and oft-visited places with unnoticed corners."

Calgary Herald, **Canada Day Special**

"(A book) to fuel the imagination . . . (with) compelling stories to inspire a visit."

"(The author) includes a historical and cultural perspective for each region (with) the people and history of a city or town as a backdrop.

Airlines Magazine

"(The) book is a nationwide adventure . . ."

"(It) puts to rest some of the preconceived notions Canadians have of their fellow Canadians . . . providing readers with a sense of history and culture that often gets lost."

Rocky Mountain Outlook

Vancouver's Vengeance

A Novel
Barry Deane Stewart

CONTENTS

CHARACTERS

Booksellers:

Jeremy Boucher	Columbus, Ohio
Chester Chalk	Vancouver, Canada
Simon Katz	New York, New York
Colin Mackenzie	London, England
Graham Maltsby	Sydney, Australia
Alan Page	Phoenix, Arizona
Stuart Scott	Toronto, Canada
Margaret Thomas	Los Angeles, California
Yrrab "Herb" Trawets	Pismo Beach, California

Book Collectors:

Ray Cartwright	President of the United States
Reginald Cushing	Deceased, Los Angeles, California
George Douglas	Deceased, Vancouver, Canada
Lord Southley	British High Commissioner to Canada
Hadrian Wall	Industrialist, Vancouver, Canada
Louis Wing	Entrepreneur, San Francisco, California

U.S. Government:

Elsie Browning	President's Executive Assistant
Maria Rodriguez	President's Personal Administrator
Sybil Stella Stephens	Director, FBI
E.Z. Wilson	Special Agent, FBI

Others:

Ian Fleming	Inspector, RCMP, Vancouver, Canada
Jonathan Robertson	History Professor, Vancouver, Canada
Gunther Shultz	Auctioneer
Nored Trawets	Herb Trawets' cousin
Mr. Wu	Chinese book broker

HISTORICAL EVENT

On April 16th and 17th, 2007, an antiquarian book auction took place at Christie's in New York. It was a landmark event in the market for rare books related to the travels and voyages of explorers from the sixteenth to early twentieth centuries.

Frank Streeter was a renowned collector of antiquarian books related to the history of maritime exploration and the science of navigation. His collection of over 550 volumes, ranging back to the 1500s, was being auctioned off. It was an excellent collection that included the published journals of many famous explorers, including Drake, Cook, Vancouver, Lewis and Clark, Champlain, and Franklin, as well as scientific publications by Darwin, Harrison, and Newton.

Due to the quality of the collection and the reputation of Streeter, Christie's pre-sale estimate was that the sale would set record-level prices and total $5 million, perhaps as much as $7 million.

The sale generated over $16 million.

BOOK ONE

The First Auction

New York Times Weekend Book Section, January 3rd

On December 27th Mr. Reginald Cushing of Los Angeles, California, passed away peacefully due to natural causes at the age of 88.

Mr. Cushing, Reggie to his friends, was the original proprietor of Knib and Kwill, a legendary antiquarian bookstore located in Hollywood. That enterprise was sold to Mr. Thaddeus Thomas a few years ago and is now operated by his daughter, Ms. Margaret Thomas.

For more than fifty years, Mr. Cushing was a leading figure in the rare-book collecting world, promoting the preservation of historically significant books and documents. He was a past president of the Antiquarian Booksellers Association of America and the International League of Antiquarian Booksellers, both of which have issued testimonials to him and have offered condolences to his family.

Mr. Cushing had an extensive personal collection of outstanding books and maps related to the history of the exploration of western and northern America. His family has announced that the collection will be sold by auction later this year, once it has been properly catalogued. Details will be provided later.

1

Hadrian Wall was sitting in his home library, looking out across the panoramic view below his home on the hillside of West Vancouver. He was contemplating a phone call he had just received from Chester Chalk, an independent dealer in rare books who had been a key advisor and supplier to Hadrian over the past ten years.

His view was spectacular. Looking down across the yacht club and ship docks on the Burrard Inlet, the long, suspended arch of the Lions Gate Bridge, and the extensive rainforest canopy of Stanley Park, Hadrian could see the impressive skyline of downtown Vancouver. Farther away, on the horizon, were the mountain peaks of the Coastal Range, dominated by the snow-capped Mount Baker in Washington. The open waters of the Strait of Juan de Fuca, leading to the Pacific Ocean, fanned out to the southwest, populated with large international freighters, gleaming cruise ships, bustling ferries, and many diverse pleasure craft, all sharing the sun-drenched expanse.

Now in his early sixties, Hadrian was very comfortable. Of medium height with slightly graying temples, he kept himself in good shape. Although he would almost always wear business suits when he went out in public, he was equally at ease in jeans when relaxing at home.

Hadrian was a semi-retired mining consultant who had been very successful over his career in identifying areas with valuable mineral deposits and parlaying that information into substantial front-end payments and ongoing royalties from large mining companies. He continued to dabble in exploration analyses and to sit on business advisory boards at some of those companies.

Looking out from his library, he could see the outline of the campus of the University of British Columbia, high up on the cliffs of Point Grey, across the intervening English Bay. He had graduated with a geology degree, followed by an MBA, from UBC some four decades ago.

After a few years working for a coal mining company in the interior mountains of British Columbia, he had ventured out on his own. He formed a loose alliance with three other independent geologists and they scoured the province for new mineral opportunities, tapping in to every information source they could find and chasing every promising lead they could define. Usually it was a dead end.

It also presented a very delicate set of relationships with his associates. They were independent entrepreneurs, both cooperating and competing at the same time. There are few situations in the world that can lead to bad feelings, lost friendships, angry lawsuits, and even mayhem and murder than those involving explorationists who believe they have been cheated out of a big discovery. Ambiguity was the source of most disputes.

Thankfully, he had never had a problem with his associates. They maintained open and cordial relationships and they were always explicit with each other as to who was in and who was out of a particular venture.

For a couple of decades they made a decent living, identifying and capitalizing on leads for coal, copper, zinc, and a few other related minerals.

Hadrian's path to financial success came in the late 1980s when he heard stories about geologists starting to believe that there could be geological formations that housed kimberlitic deposits in the northern territories of Canada. Kimberlite is the volcanic rock type that often contains diamonds. It is sourced very deep in the earth's crust, 200 miles or more down, and is usually released to the surface in narrow, carrot-shaped, pipe-like fissures that allow for rapid release of pressure and temperature. They are difficult to discover because of their relatively small size in large regions of volcanic deposits. Their potential presence can be signaled by the presence of trace amounts of associated compounds containing chromium, potassium, and magnesium.

At the time, the major sources of diamonds were in Africa, Australia, and the former Soviet Union. There was a lot of skepticism in the established mining companies, and by experienced exploration geologists as well, about the potential for diamonds in northern Canada. Hadrian was more open-minded.

Although he did not make the initial discovery of diamonds, he had worked the region very thoroughly and he had identified specific areas of potential mineralization. Once diamond discoveries had been confirmed, the rush was on to stake out claims across the Canadian Shield, the hard-rock region that stretches from northern Quebec and Ontario, across Manitoba and Saskatchewan, and into Nunavut and the Northwest Territories. Hadrian approached world-scale mining companies with his information and secured large finder's fees and ongoing royalty payments. He did not need to raise large amounts of capital or organize large operations, which were not his areas of expertise. Such ambitions often led to the failure of explorationists who made a discovery, but who could not manage the follow-up.

Canada's first diamond mine opened in 1999, and by 2003 Canada was the third-largest supplier in the world, after Botswana and Russia. Today Canada produces twenty-five percent of the world's diamonds.

Even during his earliest years exploring for minerals, Hadrian became interested in the history of mining. He read many history books about the early discoveries and the mining technologies that developed over time. He started a modest collection of early books on the subject.

For explorers and miners everywhere over the centuries, gold has always had its special allure. In 1896 gold was discovered in the Klondike region of the Yukon Territory of Canada. This is the story of legends—miners climbing the snow-filled cliffs of the Chilkoot Pass, the RCMP policing the wild mining camps and preserving the Canadian ownership of the region, and the Robert Service classics *The Shooting of Dan McGrew* and *The Cremation of Sam McGee*. The story of the region was best captured in the book *Klondike* by Pierre Berton, who was born in the Yukon and became Canada's most famous historian with over fifty very readable publications.

When Hadrian became involved with the search for diamonds in the north, he read Berton's book and then his later classic *Arctic Grail*, which describes the historic search for a northwest passage across the top of North America and the early explorers' attempts to be the first to reach the North Pole. The stories of their epic voyages, extreme hardships, and satisfying successes fascinated him. He then began to collect the early publications associated with those Arctic explorers. Over time, his interests expanded to include the exploration and discovery of the whole northwest of America.

Hadrian now had quite a comprehensive collection of old books and maps related to the subject. He had developed a network of contacts in the booksellers' world, was on many international mailing lists, and attended many antiquarian book fairs.

Chester Chalk had become one of his main sources of books and information. Chester lived in Vancouver and was an independent broker. He had worked in the book business for a number of years, originally in association with other sellers as a researcher, verifier, and sales representative. Now, he specialized in finding and reselling special volumes related to maritime exploration by maintaining an extensive network of suppliers and customers.

Chester was very different from Hadrian. A large man in his early forties, he tended to dress casually and was quite outgoing in discussions with others, whereas Hadrian was quiet-spoken, a man of few words who was precise in speech.

Hadrian and Chester got along well. Hadrian trusted Chester's advice and Chester gave him priority access to special finds. Part of their connection was that they both had a nickname that was unusual—one that close friends used and was sometimes used quietly by others, but which did not pass the test of being used easily by casual acquaintances.

Hadrian was called Stone by his friends. It had developed in university based on the fact that he was studying geology and that he was kidded by his friends that his mother had named him after a stone wall in Scotland. Thus he was often called Stone Wall. His wife stayed with Hadrian.

Chester Chalk had been called Cheese by his friends since high school days, a play on the old saying "as different as chalk and cheese." It didn't have any real meaning; it was just one of those things that happen between friends.

Hadrian was contemplating the call he had just received from Chester. The famous collection of books related to maritime history owned by Reggie Cushing was going to auction.

They needed a plan of action.

2

Jeremy Boucher was in his Antiquarian Americana shop on High Street, near Ohio State University in Columbus. January was always a slow time, after the busy pre-Christmas rush of December when buyers seemed to be keen on adding to their collections and the gift-giving nature of the season kicked in. Now, in the gray and gloomy winter season, it was time to take stock and to plan his book purchasing ventures of the next few months.

He was reading the announcement of the upcoming sale of Reggie Cushing's collection of antiquarian books and maps.

Jeremy had a thriving business in the purchase and sale of antiquarian books related to American history. Although his main focus was on the history of eastern America and the Civil War, he had expanded to more western America items in recent years. He regularly attended the antiquarian book fairs in California and Seattle, and he had developed a reasonable base of customers who were interested in items related to that region.

Jeremy's specialty was in items of high quality. He was almost fanatical about the condition of old books, their absolute originality and completeness, and any special provenance of previous ownership. Other booksellers often laughed behind his back about his obsession with quality, but, on the other hand, his customers knew they were always getting the best, even if it was at a premium price.

Jeremy was always well-dressed and immaculately groomed. Tall and slim, in his early fifties, he spoke softly in serious tones. His appearance was totally consistent with his character and reputation.

Jeremy knew that Reginald Cushing's collection was of the highest quality; he had often interacted with Reggie at book fairs and industry association events.

However, he also knew that everyone in the antiquarian-book-collecting world knew the same thing. How could he find an opportunity at the auction, which was undoubtedly not going to occur until the fall, given the auction house's task of collating the collection, preparing an appropriate sales catalogue, and building market expectations?

Jeremy could think of a number of approaches, some of which were not in conflict with each other and some of which would create significant conflicts of interest. He also knew that others would be considering the exact same options.

First, he could simply bid for specific items for his own account, adding to his inventory and hoping to re-sell the items within a reasonable time at a profit. Although this was his traditional approach to auctions, this time it was a high-risk approach with limited chance of real value creation. This particular auction was going to attract everyone's attention—the big dealers and the serious collectors alike. His only hope with this strategy would be to be able to recognize some items of exceptional value because of their quality, rarity, or special provenance. Because of his expertise, this strategy was possible for an item or two, but it was not likely to create many opportunities.

The second approach would be to identify individuals within his customer network who would be interested in some of the items in the auction, to work with them on an auction strategy, and to actually carry out the bidding process for them, for a fee of course. This was a common practice for the many auctions in London, New York, and a few other major centers. Collectors, even high-value ones, did not usually have the time or willingness to monitor the many auctions to find a specific item of interest. That's where the experience and the network of contacts for a world-class dealer like Jeremy came into play.

The inherent problem with this second strategy as related to a big event such as the Cushing auction was to avoid creating conflicts of interest. He could not be bidding on something for more than one person, let alone be considering buying for himself at the same time. However, if he was pursuing this strategy with a number of buyers, which was the best way to have multiple profit opportunities, how could he avoid having more than one of his clients interested in the same item?

The third approach was to form an alliance with another quality bookseller or two. This was normal in the industry when items of high value were involved. It shared the cost, and therefore the risk. It also expanded the reach to potential customers if you associated with dealers who had a different network. Obviously, it also served to reduce the competition at the auction. For Jeremy, the problem was that he did not have such an established relationship with other appropriate dealers; he was a bit of an outsider in those circles. However, he knew very well that others would be doing just that.

There was a fourth approach. It was based on history and opportunity, but it was unproven to him.

In 2007, when the now-famous Streeter collection of antiquarian books related to maritime exploration was auctioned in New York, everyone was surprised by the price levels that were reached. Over three sessions, 550 books were sold for a total value of over $16 million. The pre-sale estimates had ranged from $5 million to $7 million, even allowing for the quality of the collection and the booming financial markets of the time.

The three sessions of the auction were held at 6:00 p.m. on a Monday and at 10:00 a.m. and 2:00 p.m. on Tuesday. The lots were auctioned at a rate of slightly more than one minute each! The individual items sold for an average price of $30,000 compared to an estimate of $10,000. Thirty-five books sold for over $100,000 and four sold for over $500,000. Everyone was shocked.

The sale catalogue had listed the books alphabetically. The very first item to be auctioned was an English translation of a relatively obscure treatise on the West Indies by a Spanish missionary named Acosta, printed in 1604. Its pre-sale price was estimated by Christie's at $3,000 to $4,000. It sold for over $15,000. The tone of the sale was set! By the end of the first evening session, 150 books had sold for almost $4 million, more than twice the estimate.

In 2007, although information on the internet at sales sites such as eBay and Amazon was well established, the antiquarian book world use of it was still in its infancy. Sites such as Abe Books and Book Finder were established and some booksellers were using them, but it was still hit-and-miss. Inside knowledge of who had specific books was still often dependent upon relationships, book fair connections, and scouting.

In reality, only a limited number of the high-end dealers and a random selection of other dealers and collectors were at the Streeter Sale. Thus, there was a significant market discontinuity of information about the emerging prices within the world of antiquarian booksellers for a day or two.

Dealers, particularly those that belong to the established professional associations such as the Antiquarian Booksellers Association of America (ABAA) or the International League of Antiquarian Booksellers (ILAB), have an understanding that members will sell books to each other at a 10 to 20 percent discount from their asking retail price.

This practice is more than a professional courtesy. The market for expensive, rare books is not a liquid one—inventory turnover can be slow. It has been said by the insiders many times, "A $100,000 book only exists if there is a $100,000 customer." Thus booksellers covet their relationships with collectors. They look for opportunities to buy a book at 80 or 90 percent of retail value from another dealer and then turn it over relatively quickly to a customer they know is in the market for the item.

Astute collectors certainly know this. They come to expect discounts of at least 10 percent from dealers with whom they deal regularly. As well, if they locate a book they want in the inventory of a dealer who won't give them a discount, they simply arrange for a friendly dealer to buy it at a 20 percent discount and they split the savings.

Of course, all of this means that the original purchase of the book by the first bookseller has to be at 50 or 60 percent of retail value in order to provide any room for profit on the resale. This was becoming harder and harder to achieve as the internet listing of books became more prevalent and the market became more transparent.

However, when a market discontinuity occurs, as it did with the Streeter sale, knowledge creates opportunities. Starting in the morning of the second day of the Streeter Sale, well before the second session even commenced, astute buyers who recognized the significance of the previous evening's price levels worked their computers and telephones to purchase key books from other unaware sources, obviously at the pre-Streeter prices, even without pushing for the maximum discounts that were usually available.

Over the forty-eight hours following the first sales of the auction, many books were bought and sold off-line. Predictably, this resulted in some very bad feelings, lost relationships and friendships, and even some reneging of book deliveries by some of the sellers as they became aware of the Streeter results. In this case it was "Seller Beware!"—a reversal of the normal admonition.

The issue that Jeremy was mulling was whether or not the Cushing sale would present similar opportunities and how he could profit from them.

3

Jeremy Boucher was not the only dealer contemplating the Cushing auction. Other dealers, worldwide, were having similar thoughts.

Simon Katz, in New York, is one of the leading rare-book sellers in the world. Simon had been one of the primary buyers at the Streeter Sale, in partnership with two other dealers from the Northeast. They had driven the prices up to new heights.

At the time, it was considered a high-risk move, but they had decided that the good economic times and the emergence of wealthy, soon-to-retire baby boomers who were looking for new interests such as rare-book collecting provided the right opportunity. As well as making some good investments, the maneuver in effect doubled the value of their extensive inventories, worth millions of dollars.

The question was whether or not a similar opportunity was going to be available with the Cushing auction. It was one thing to bid up prices and apparent values; it was another to actually have the general market respond to such moves and sustain itself at the new levels.

It was somewhat surprising to everyone that, even after the financial market meltdown of 2008, the market for rare books did not back off from the 2007 Streeter values. In fact, many prices grew well beyond the Streeter sale level over the next few years.

Simon was not afraid to make breakout moves in the market, but he did wonder if the current market had any capacity for significant upward movement. Just because the magnificent Cushing collection was coming on the market didn't mean that the Streeter situation was going to repeat itself.

He needed to do some careful planning and to test the perceptions of his associates who joined up with him last time. A mistake could cost him a lot of money.

In London, Colin Mackenzie was considering the same things. London is the epicenter of the antiquarian-book world, somewhat based on history and somewhat due to its being at the crossroads of international travel. Certainly New York had captured a lot of business over the last century, but it was still a reality that Americans tended to focus on their own areas of interest—their history, geography, authors, and political developments. The world of antiquarian books is so much more.

Western Europeans generally have taken a broader interest, partially driven by the fact that much of the history between the fifteenth and nineteenth centuries in the Americas, Africa, and the Far East was driven by European explorers and conquerors. That is the period of antiquarian books.

The development of open markets in Russia and Eastern Europe, China, and even South America has expanded the availability of valuable old books and created new wealthy collectors.

Significant variations in currency exchange rates over the past two decades have also impacted the markets. The falloff in the value of the U.S dollar due to the country's economic and political problems caused a real buyers' market for Europeans for a while. But then, the European Union financial issues and the woes of the Euro tipped things back again. Dealers saw their inventory values and the attitudes of their international customers fluctuate wildly.

Interestingly, countries such as Canada and Australia saw a general strengthening of their currencies and so collectors there who were interested in subjects such as Pacific and Arctic exploration found new purchasing opportunities and actually caused those values to increase noticeably in terms of U.S. dollars or Euros.

Colin was very familiar with the Cushing collection and he knew it was of high value and would attract a lot of attention. But, what did that really mean in terms of competition, prices, and opportunities?

In Toronto, Stuart Scott pondered how he would approach the Cushing auction. As a specialized bookseller, he focused on rare books related to the exploration of the Arctic and Antarctic—the voyages of Franklin, Ross, Parry, Rae, Amundsen, Peary, etc. It was a popular field, especially among Canadian collectors, and he had developed a good network of clients. Although he would need to manage his different customer relationships carefully, he believed that motivated collectors always had an advantage over dealers at an auction—they thought in terms of retail prices while the dealers had to think in terms of wholesale prices and resale potential. Therefore, all things being equal, a customer should be able to bid 25 percent or more above a dealer, which would leave room for Stuart to collect 10 percent or more from a customer as a commission for advising him on auction tactics.

Of course, high profile auctions were always a bit of a crapshoot. As the saying went, "Auctions just prove the Greater Fool Theory," meaning that the winner was the one who was willing to pay too much, whether due to ignorance, ego, or just getting caught up in the excitement of the auction.

In Sydney, Graham Maltsby was contemplating the same issues as Stuart Scott, with a somewhat different focus on subject matter. His client network tended to collect books related to the early exploration of the Pacific Ocean—Magellan, Cook, La Perouse, Anson, Vancouver, etc. These explorers were the first to define the South Pacific, including Australia and New Zealand. The strengthening of the Australian dollar over the past decade gave the local collectors a sense of confidence in their competitiveness as world prices had come down significantly in terms of their money. As with the Canadian dollar, Australian exchange rates that had been around sixty cents U.S. to the dollar were now near par or even better.

In Los Angeles, Margaret Thomas had another approach. She now operated the Knib and Kwill Book Shop in Hollywood. It was the business that Reginald Cushing had established decades ago and which he had sold to Margaret's father, Thaddeus Thomas, a few years back. Her father had passed away last year, coincidentally a short time before Cushing.

As a result of that history, Margaret had a thorough understanding of the Cushing collection that was coming up for sale. She also had a personal link to the Cushing family, which she had hoped would have given her an inside track to purchase the collection or, at least, to be the advisor and organizer for its sale. Even though it required a fair amount of work to organize a major auction, the sales organization collected as much as 25 percent of the value, which would be a lot of money in this case.

However, the family had rejected her offer, deciding instead to consign the sale to a major auction house with offices in New York and London.

They had explained that they believed that the auction house had a deeper expertise and broader reach. They also thought, without explicitly telling her so, that they preferred to have Margaret as a potential purchaser at the auction—she represented a valuable constituency.

To their credit, the family was right in that latter assessment. Margaret, spurred on by her irritation at not being chosen to lead the sale, was motivated to be an active participant. She was a determined woman; in fact, behind her back others in the industry often called her the Iron Lady, a not-too-subtle reference to the sound-alike-named Margaret Thatcher.

Margaret's hole card in the upcoming auction was her relationship with Louis Wing.

4

Louis Wing was an avid book collector. He had just finished a conversation with Margaret Thomas about the Cushing book collection. With a smile of anticipation on his face, he was looking forward to the upcoming auction. Louis was a man of action and he liked to take control of situations. How could he do that here? How could he improve his chances?

Louis was very rich, having made his fortune creating software for very high resolution video images on phones. Typical of the many Silicon Valley high-technology success stories, he had started in modest facilities with a small staff and had created something ahead of the curve for the booming electronics and communication industries. Once he had established the viability of his creation and had developed credibility with the large manufacturers, he didn't follow the pattern of launching his own public company. He had seen too many great successes flame out as they couldn't duplicate their success on an ongoing basis. Instead he sold the rights to his technology to an established firm. He realized $100 million up front from that deal and he still received ongoing royalties from the applications of the technology and his associated patents.

Since Louis was a very ambitious and proactive individual, many people were surprised that he had sold his business rather than expand it. Some of them even called him Chicken, but only behind his back.

Despite his success, Louis didn't have a big ego. In fact, he had a good sense of humour and in private didn't take himself too seriously. He was amused to learn that some folks would call him Chicken Wing. "Just a big, plump, rich bird, I guess," he would say with a big laugh, also alluding to his large size. He was in his early 50s, six feet tall and weighed 230 pounds. His dark-black hair, cut rather short, emphasized his parents' Chinese heritage. He had never married.

Louis lived in San Francisco. Having created his success in the Silicon Valley, this was a bit of an anomaly. Most of the people in the high-tech industries, including the lawyers and financial executives, not just the technical people, tended to live in San Jose and throughout the Santa Clara Valley.

Although he was quite outgoing in business and social settings, and even dressed with a stylish flare, he also enjoyed his private times. He felt there was a certain anonymity that came with living in the city rather than the valley. He had a home not far from the top of Lombard Street in central San Francisco, the street known as the most crooked street in the world, with its eight hairpin turns going down the hill in a one-block span. He enjoyed being able to walk to the city attractions and restaurants in privacy.

He certainly hadn't developed a large public profile, whether in social issues such as Bill Gates, sports team ownership such as Paul Allen, or politics such as Ray Cartwright.

He had actually met Ray Cartwright some years ago. He was attending a large conference of executives and entrepreneurs from new technology companies and he had been in a discussion group with him. At that time, Ray Cartwright was the president of a company that had created a breakout financial reporting system. The company was called Ticker Treat. It was very different in technology from what Louis was doing, but many of the development and marketing challenges were similar. Ray and Louis hit it off well.

Over drinks at one of the conference cocktail receptions, Ray Cartwright had shared his passion for the history of the discovery of western America and his collecting of antiquarian books and maps related to that era. Ray's enthusiasm resonated with Louis and, as a result, he followed up to learn more about the subject. Over the last ten years he had become a dedicated collector himself.

He had started with the early exploration of the North American Southwest, since that was where he had grown up and where he still lived. Much of that history is linked to the Spanish activities from the 1500s until the mid-1800s. One thing he discovered was that the Spanish had been very secretive about their exploration and discoveries, and so original materials were hard to obtain. That made any items that did surface very valuable.

Over time, his interests expanded to include all of Pacific North America. He now possessed one of the largest collections related to that, one that he believed even rivalled Ray Cartwright's.

Of course, Ray Cartwright wasn't very active collecting books these days. He was kept rather busy being President of the United States.

5

It was a bright, sunny mid-February Friday afternoon in Los Angeles, one that locals would call a Chamber of Commerce day. The California Antiquarian Book Fair was about to open in the Pasadena Convention Center.

This annual three-day fair alternates every other year between Los Angeles and San Francisco. The Los Angeles fairs have been held in Pasadena since 2012, a change from the many years it was held in a hotel ballroom in West Hollywood.

The new venue is more spacious for the dealers and more accessible for travellers. It also has more close-by amenities. Colorado Avenue is filled with upscale shops and restaurants. Attractions such as the Huntington Library and Art Gallery, the Rose Bowl, and the campus of Cal Tech offer visitors sightseeing options.

The fair attracts a few thousand attendees over the three days. That's not a large group by normal business conference standards, but almost all of them are potential customers for the dealers. There will be a few academics, researchers, and curiosity lookers. Some of the collectors will be there for many hours, all three days, looking for some sought-after treasure on the book-filled shelves of the dealers.

Over two hundred high-quality booksellers, all members of ABAA or ILAB, had been assembling their display booths since the previous day.

There are two different sizes of booth spaces. Three-quarters of them are 10' by 10'; the rest are 10' by 15'. Of course, the rental rate reflects the difference. The larger spaces are typically taken by the large book dealers from New York or London, although sometimes two dealers share a space. This reduces costs and also allows dealers who do not have large inventories to combine their materials and create a more attractive image for the customers who would be walking up and down the aisles, perusing the various offerings.

Each dealer has a personal layout for his or her space, using various combinations of book cases, tables, signs, draped dividers, and glass topped display cases. These latter items are usually situated at the front of the booth space against the walking aisle with the dealer's most attractive or most unusual items in them, designed to catch a customer's eye.

The booksellers' specialties cover a wide range of subjects: literature, history, science, biographies, comic books, maps and atlases, whatever might interest collectors. Booths are assigned to dealers randomly by a draw and so various dealers with a similar specialty are scattered throughout the large convention hall. Sometimes major competitors are widely separated; sometimes they are right beside each other.

Each booth usually has at least two people staffing it, the dealer plus a partner, spouse, employee, or a friend. This helps to handle the busy times when there are hundreds of people browsing through the hall and when there could be a half dozen people shuffling around each other looking at the displayed books in the relatively small booth spaces. It also provides relief from the long hours of standing—the book fair runs for twenty hours over the three days. And, it allows the dealers to delegate most of the initial setup to someone else as they browse around the other booths in the time before the book fair actually opens to the public.

Many books are sold between dealers in this preliminary period. In fact, some dealers consider that opportunity as being a major factor in their decision to attend book fairs.

Individual booksellers can be experts in only so many areas and will have a customer base that generally reflects that. However, in their sourcing of books, say by buying private collections or being offered books by people who contact them directly, they obtain a wide range of titles. They typically bring their most interesting ones to the book fairs. That's why dealers aggressively scout each other, looking for books in their own specialty area that some other bookseller may have acquired. Often that other dealer will not fully appreciate the value of a book if it has some particular aspect that makes it unique. Taking advantage of the 20 percent discount that dealers give to each other, it is not uncommon for one dealer to buy a book from someone in this period and to put it in his own display and sell it for twice the amount to a customer when the fair opens to the public.

This is considered fair game and is quite normal within the booksellers' world. Of course, the first dealer has also made a profit on the book that he bought cheaper in the first place. This practice is even more prevalent at the various regional book fairs that take place across the country all year long. There, local booksellers, who usually do not belong to the ABAA, gather in similar setups. ABAA members who reside in the area often scoop up books from those dealers and take them on to the larger book fairs such as Los Angeles and New York. For example, during the week before this Los Angeles fair there was a regional fair in San Francisco that attracted about two hundred sellers, but only twenty of them were also here in L.A. this week.

Simon Katz, Margaret Thomas, Jeremy Boucher, Colin Mackenzie, and Graham Maltsby, among many others, were mingling around the booths, greeting the many people they knew. Most of these dealers would see each other at least a half-dozen times a year at various venues across North America and Europe. Most of them purchased a book or two during their rounds.

Jeremy was somewhat amused to note that no one had mentioned the Cushing auction in their initial contacts. He was sure there would be lots of chats about the event, likely somewhat tenuously, over the next three days as people mingled more casually or encountered each other in various receptions or bars. Everyone would be curious to know what others were planning to do while no one would want to share their own ideas. Much would be said, but little would be divulged.

6

The doors to the book fair opened precisely at 3:00 p.m. The few hundred people who had been waiting in line for that moment surged in and spread out through the convention hall.

Hadrian Wall, who had been in the outer foyer waiting for the opening, held back for a few moments. He was always amused by the early rush, because once people were inside they slowed down and started to saunter up the various aisles. It wasn't as if this was Wal-Mart or Best Buy on Black Friday after Thanksgiving when everyone rushed to seize advertised bargains. Here, the search for desirable purchases was going to be slow and methodical. Except where someone spotted a very specific item they were searching for, actual purchase decisions often involved a number of visits to a given booth and a series of conversations with the dealer that could spread out over the three days of the fair. Buyers usually checked out all of the offerings in their areas of interest before committing to purchases. Like everyone else in the business, they were always on the lookout for the good deal—the book that had been overlooked or underpriced by everyone else.

Hadrian knew most of the dealers who dealt in books and maps related to world exploration, and particularly the history of northern and western America. He greeted them by name and looked over their racks of books.

Most of the dealers called him Hadrian, but a few who knew him particularly well, such as Stuart Scott from Toronto, called him Stone. Colin Mackenzie from London, always proper, called him Mr. Wall.

He hadn't seen Stuart for a few months and so he drifted in his direction early in the session. He had purchased many books from Stuart over the years, usually related to the exploration of the Canadian Arctic.

"Hi, Stuart. How is it going?"

"Hey, Stone. Great to see you. When did you get down here?"

"Oh, I flew down from Vancouver last night. I'll be staying through the weekend and then heading over to Palm Desert for a few days of golf. How about you?"

"I flew from Toronto to San Francisco last week for the regional book fair there, and then, after browsing for a few days in the Napa Valley wine country, I headed down here. I'll be going back to Toronto on Monday."

"What's new?" asked Hadrian, the code for finding out about any new books that Stuart had, not an interest in any more details of Stuart's travels or personal life.

"Well, I have a few things that might interest you, a couple of which I did pick up in San Francisco last week.

"First of all, there is a great set of Sir John Richardson's four volumes, the *Fauna Boreali-Americana—the Zoology of Northern British America*. Richardson was the naturalist who traveled with Sir John Franklin on his overland expeditions to the Arctic in the 1820s. He meticulously described the habitat and physical characteristics of numerous species, many for the first time. The first volume describes 82 quadrupeds; the second, 238 birds; the third, 133 fish; and the fourth, 447 insects. All the volumes have amazing sketches, many in vivid color. This is a spectacular set. Many people compare Richardson's work to that of Audubon, who came later.

"What makes the set of Richardsons so valuable is that they are very hard to find. The four volumes were issued over eight years from 1829 to 1837 by four different publishers. Due to the economic situation of the times, they were not a good seller then, and, as a result, each successive volume was printed in smaller amounts. To find all four volumes in excellent condition is very unusual; the fish and insect volumes are particularly hard to find. You can see that they have been re-bound in classic leather covers with high-quality embossing and very colorful end papers. These are special."

Hadrian picked up each of the volumes and flipped through the pages. The books were in excellent shape and the illustrations were as crisp and clear as one could imagine.

"How much would they be, Stuart?"

"For you, $25,000. That's a good price."

"What else do you have to show me?"

Over the next twenty minutes Stuart showed Hadrian a handful of other books. Hadrian already had a couple of them, having purchased them from Chester Chalk since he had last talked to Stuart. The others were not of particular interest to him, usually related to minor excursions to the Arctic that were not very historic in nature, or books that were not in excellent condition.

He returned to the Richardson set. When discussing sales with dealers, Hadrian and the dealer would normally conduct a minor negotiation. As a reputable collector and as a good or potentially valuable future customer, dealers would usually offer him a 10 percent discount, sometimes a bit more. However, with Scott, he already had a long term relationship and

Scott had already offered him a discount price. His "For you . . ." comment was not just some salesman patter, it was genuine.

"OK, let's do it," said Hadrian.

Security at a large, very busy book fair, with hundreds of people milling about handling small items that can be worth tens of thousands of dollars, can be a concern. It would be easy to tuck a book away in a bag or coat pocket.

Therefore, no one other than accredited dealers can bring a book into the sales area, and every book that is taken out must be placed in a transparent plastic bag with a colorful bag tag and sales slip attached with the selling dealer's name and booth number displayed. It's a primitive system but it seems to work, although there are always instances where a determined thief can abscond with a valuable book.

Hadrian walked off with his four volumes safely ensconced in a large plastic bag. If he didn't want to carry it with him during the day, he could deposit it at the security desk for safekeeping.

An observer would also have noticed that Hadrian did not pay Stuart for the books. For such an established customer, Stuart would send Hadrian a detailed invoice in the next week, probably by e-mail, and Hadrian would send payment at the end of the month.

The antiquarian book world operates on good faith much of the time. It is normal to send valuable books to customers anywhere in the world for their inspection, with payment or their return accepted later without question. Bad faith or bad credit is seldom a problem—an amazing thing in today's world.

7

Louis Wing was also wandering through the book fair. He was casually dressed, as was almost everyone, but Louis was definitely noticeable. His large figure, Chinese heritage, brightly-patterned shirt, and colored Italian leather shoes stood out. He conveyed a presence, even though he hardly spoke. The crowd of fellow book-browsers noticed him, to be sure, but they had no idea who he was. In spite of his wealth, he was a relatively unknown figure publicly, even in California.

That was certainly not the case with the major booksellers. Louis was a big collector and they all wanted to deal with him. If this were the world of gambling in Las Vegas or Monte Carlo, Louis would be called a whale. Here, he was called Louis by those he had relationships with and Mr. Wing by the others. No one here called him Chicken!

He approached the Knib and Kwill booth and saw that Margaret Thomas was there, holding court with a small cluster of people.

Margaret was easy to spot. In her mid-forties, she was quite tall and slim, always had an eye-catching style to her long, blonde hair, and dressed in fashionable suits, usually in bright colors. Today, she was decked out in bright yellow.

As Louis hung back a little and observed the group around Margaret, he quickly deduced that it included a couple of newspaper reporters and the manager of the book fair, along with a public affairs assistant. Obviously the fair was hoping to generate some coverage in the Saturday papers that would attract more people to the event.

Margaret's latest statement seemed to indicate that the interview was wrapping up. "Yes, the Los Angeles book fair is a major happening in the world of antiquarian books. There are over two hundred leading dealers here and there will be a few thousand attendees over the three days. Valuable and rare books, some worth almost a million dollars, are here for anyone to see. It's all very exciting."

Louis could tell from the body language that the manager of the fair was very pleased with that statement. Margaret was a good ambassador for the industry.

Just as the group was starting to break up, one of the reporters spoke up. "Just one more question, if I could. Would you comment for our readers about the upcoming auction of rare books from the Cushing collection? I understand it will be a big deal."

After only a minor pause, Margaret said, "Sure. The Cushing collection of antiquarian books relating to maritime exploration and the discovery of western America is one of the best in the world. It includes some unique volumes that seldom surface in the marketplace. I'm sure that the auction will attract a great deal of attention from buyers who would like to acquire such special items."

"Do you expect that prices will be high?"

"Unique items always attract interest. I would not be surprised to see some aggressive bidding. High prices are a relative thing, based on an item's interest to buyers, rarity, and quality. We'll see."

"Thanks."

After the group had moved on, Louis walked over to the booth and greeted Margaret. "Hi, it looks like you are the star attraction of the fair," he said with a smile on his face.

"Hi, Louis," she responded. "I didn't see you there. You know, the fair people are always looking to generate some publicity and I don't mind giving them a hand. They do a good job organizing this event."

"I agree; they sure do."

"Have you wandered around much yet?"

"No, I just got here and thought I would start with you," he replied.

Then, knowing full well that Margaret would have been scouting out the other major dealers before the fair opened, he continued, "Did you find anything lately that would be of interest to me?"

"Perhaps. I think you are somewhat familiar with the journeys of the British naval officer William Broughton. He was a senior officer with George Vancouver on his famous voyage around the world and he participated in the detailed mapping of the northwest coast of America. He had been sent back to Britain by Vancouver in 1793 to obtain more explicit instructions from the government. Then in 1795, Broughton captained his own voyage around the world that lasted for over four years. He explored new areas of Asia, Japan, the South Pacific, and the coast of North America. His exploits were the basis for Britain's claim to the Oregon Territory fifty years later.

"His journal was published in 1804 but in very limited quantities. Thus it is an important and scarce document for a collector such as you to have."

"I certainly have the journals of many explorers from that era. I generally recall Broughton's involvement with Vancouver from reading some of the accounts of Vancouver's adventures, but I hadn't realized that he had undertaken his own significant voyage."

After looking through the journal, bound in bold red leather, and noting its excellent condition, he went through the drill of setting the price with Margaret. Unlike the simple routine that Hadrian Wall had gone through with Stuart Scott, Margaret led Louis through a summary of other such books that had been sold at auction in the past few years and which had been listed on bookseller internet sites. This was all designed to show Louis that her asking price of $30,000 was a good one. Louis agreed.

After that exchange, Louis wandered away to check out the other booksellers. He knew that he would find a few items of interest; he always did. They might be minor items or books tucked into the shelves of dealers who specialized in other areas, but they were always there to be found. Sometimes a dealer would add to his display after the fair was under way for a couple of hours, having kept some books back from the prying eyes of other dealers, so they could avoid discounting items they believed had good retail sales potential. That was a big part of the fun in coming to the fair in the first place. The hunt was as satisfying as the find!

Coincidentally, due to the random draw for booth locations, Simon Katz had his setup in the booth across the aisle from Margaret Thomas.

Simon and Margaret could not be more different personally and yet, within the dynamics of the book world, they were perhaps the most alike. He was in New York; she was in Los Angeles. They both had large operations and were the leaders in their areas. Both of them wanted to take charge of situations and to influence results. Both of them had a deep stable of loyal customers, although, in reality, many large collectors dealt with both of them frequently. That just intensified their competitiveness.

Simon was much more reserved in his dealings with other people. In his fifties, he was dressed in a conservative gray suit, the same color as his hair. He talked slowly and calmly, even when he was in the midst of a tough negotiation. Margaret was more dynamic and more direct with others, even when she was just deciding who should buy coffee.

They were always very polite and courteous with each other. They each respected the other as a professional competitor; there was no animosity between them.

Simon drifted across the aisle.

"Hello, Margaret. I guess the Hollywood gang has moved on. You always seem to handle them so well. The rest of us get tongue-tied or end up rambling on about details and technicalities."

"Hello, Simon. You underestimate yourself. Welcome back to California. It's certainly a great day to be here. Did you see those clear, blue skies and feel the warmth in the air this afternoon?"

"Right, just like New York except for the sunlight and the temperatures," replied Simon with a chuckle.

They both smiled.

"How's business?" she asked.

This wasn't just a casual question between dealers, nor was it a probe into his personal situation. Major players in the market were always seeking to know what was happening generally, and they usually were willing to share their perspectives. Their world was affected by the general economy, international relations, currency exchange rates, the emotional attitudes of wealthy people who were their real customers, and political developments that affected all of those things. They were in those situations together, quite independent from their own book inventories and business dealings.

Simon tended to travel more than Margaret. He certainly spent more time in London and in continental Europe. She did want to hear what he had to say.

"Things are pretty good," he said. "The economy is doing OK, and there seems to be more optimism now with President Cartwright's leadership. Of course, for us, it's always the heavy hitters that matter. In the east, the investment bankers and stock market traders always have money, as do the high-tech developers and Hollywood celebrities in your west coast market.

"The Europeans are more optimistic as well. Currencies seem to have stabilized, which takes out some of the nervousness we saw a while back. We know how disjointed the markets became over the past ten years, starting with the economic and political problems we had here in the States, which saw our dollar lose a lot of purchasing power. Then there was the Euro crisis as the various European countries such as Greece, Spain, Italy, and Cyprus struggled with their economies. Our business is truly international in scope and those discontinuities disrupt the markets.

"The current stability helps our sales. However, it does increase the competition within the industry for buying books for resale. Even the Australians and Canadians are now determined buyers."

"Those are astute observations. Thanks. I don't travel as much outside the country but what I hear is consistent. What I find interesting is that, out here, the Hollywood people seem more in tune with what's happening than the financial and technology people. I think it's because they get immediate feedback from movie attendance, DVD sales, TV advertising, etc. The financial guys just seem to believe their own opinions and forecasts. The technology guys are in an isolated world of their own—just create a successful new product and money flows no matter what else is going on."

"Right. I heard you say to the reporter that you expect the Cushing auction to attract a lot of attention. I'm sure you are right."

"I have to believe it. I know the Cushing family, and the auction house will build up the event as much as they can," she said with a touch of envy.

8

Alan Page ambled along the aisles, greeting many of the dealers, often stopping to chat for a while.

Alan was a book dealer but he didn't have a booth at the fair. He had done that up until a few years ago, but he had decided that he couldn't be profitable with that approach. He didn't have the necessary working capital or stock to take on the bigger players in the increasingly competitive market.

Alan had reverted to the tactics he used when he first entered the business. He focused on finding individual books that had some special attribute and on selling them quickly to private collectors or even other dealers. Thus, he did not need to tie up a lot of money in inventory.

Within the industry, Alan's approach was called book scouting. It usually applied to people who scoured the cheaper bookstores looking to find books that could be levered up to other sellers for a few dollars. Alan just did it at a much higher level. That's why he liked to privately refer to himself as the Eagle Scout.

Alan's appearance was consistent with that role. In an earlier period, he had been an appliance and a car salesman; that image suited his purpose. In his late forties, he was six feet tall and a bit stocky. He had relatively long, flowing blondish hair and typically wore a sports jacket with open-neck, colorful shirts. If he wore a tie, it would be in a bright, almost-clashing color, certainly in a bold pattern.

Whenever he thought back about his business successes, he always recalled the sale he made a couple of years back to Ray Cartwright, now the President of the United States but who was the Vice President then. He had earned a $200,000 commission for selling a book that no one had ever heard of, that he had never even touched, from an unknown seller he never met. All he knew was that the book was somehow related to the famous voyage of Sir Francis Drake in the 1500s. That was the strangest thing he had ever been involved with.

Alan was successful because he had developed an amazing network of contacts in both the sellers' and the collectors' worlds, one that even big players such as Simon Katz could not match. He traveled extensively, particularly to cities outside the mainstream in America and Europe and now, even more, to Eastern Europe and Asia. Those areas might not have world-leading booksellers, but they had many avid collectors, a great source for buying as well as selling valuable books.

Alan spotted Jeremy Boucher in his booth and approached him.

"Hi, Jeremy."

"Hello there, Alan. Good to see you here."

"I drove over from Phoenix this morning. I always like to see what's going on at the big fairs. How are you?"

"Fine. The fair seems to be off to a good start. I think there are more people here this year than last year."

As they chatted, Alan scanned the books that Jeremy had on display, not an unusual thing to do in these circumstances. He didn't see anything of immediate interest to him, but he didn't really expect to.

However, he had another reason to seek out Jeremy.

"I have found something that might be of interest to you. I know you have a special focus on materials related to the Civil War and like high quality material.

"During my review of a private collection of old maps and charts last week I came across some Civil War era publications. There was a bound collection of the first ten years of *Harper's Weekly*, 1857 to 1866. As you know, Harper's was the first American illustrated periodical. It has articles, maps, and illustrations related to the war and the politics of the time, including the Lincoln assassination.

"More significantly, from a collector's point of view, there are copies of Homer Winslow's two publications of drawings of soldiers and their life in the war: *Campaign Sketches* in 1863 and *Life in Camp* in 1864. The sketches first appeared in a rough form in those volumes of *Harper's Weekly*.

"These are historically significant items and they are in excellent condition. I checked the online and auction sales history of these publications for the past couple of years and I found some that were in just OK condition that collectively sold for almost $100,000. I'm sure these high quality versions will be worth much more, especially grouped together."

Jeremy was totally silent as Alan related his story, taking it all in. It was not unusual for one dealer to join up with another to buy valuable items. It was also usual for a dealer who had identified a buying opportunity to keep its source confidential to start with. He didn't have much experience in dealing with Alan, but he knew this approach was consistent with Alan's reputation of scouting out a book and flipping its sale quickly. Nothing could be faster that selling something before you actually bought it.

"What did you have in mind?" he asked.

"Well, I could resell it to you and then you can work your market independently. Or we could buy it together and share the ultimate resale profit."

"Do you have any preference?" Jeremy asked with a small smile.

"Candidly, I would prefer the first option as it avoids my tying up funds and happens more quickly. I think you know that is my style," Alan responded honestly.

"The books certainly sound interesting, especially if they're in excellent condition, as I would judge them. Can you give me some numbers?"

Alan had done his homework. He had showed the internet listing history of the books to the current owners and had explained that those values were asking prices and that actual sales usually went at a 20 percent discount. He also explained that dealers such as him needed to make a profit, and that it often took a long time to find an interested buyer, which they understood. He had a tentative deal to buy the books for $60,000, which was a surprising and welcome amount for the owners, who had bought the publications years earlier at a small fraction of that amount.

He also presumed that a dealer such as Jeremy, with his reputation and connections with serious collectors, could resell the books for $120,000 or more. Thus, if he could sell the books to Jeremy for $80,000 to $90,000, he would make a good profit without exposing any of his own money, and he would leave the potential higher value for Jeremy to capture given the uncertainty and time involved.

"I believe I can get the books for no more than $70,000. I would sell them to you for $90,000," he said, sort of telling the truth.

Jeremy thought through the offer. He knew that Alan had probably hedged his position somewhat. However, if the books were of high quality he could probably sell them for over $125,000, maybe even $140,000. He knew some customers who would be interested. He didn't have a problem with Alan making a profit, as long as he would make one as well.

"It's possible we could sell them for $110,000 to $120,000 to the right customer," Jeremy replied, playing the same game.

He continued, "I would be happy to do a joint venture with you if you want. For me to buy them outright, I can give you $85,000," calling Alan's semi-bluff he believed.

After a pause, and with a smile, Alan said, "OK."

They both felt they had made a good deal, the best test there is for an outcome.

9

The second day of the Los Angeles book fair opened with a bit of a stir among the dealers. Everyone had seen the weekend edition of the *Los Angeles Times*, in particular the Books section.

As the manager of the fair had hoped, there was a lead article about antiquarian books and the fair in progress. It was the headline and opening paragraph that caught everyone's attention.

High Prices Expected at Unique Book Sale screamed the headline. The opening paragraph went on:

"We'll see relatively high prices at the upcoming auction of Reginald Cushing's unique collection of antiquarian books," said Margaret Thomas, owner of the prestigious *Knib and Kwill* bookstore, interviewed at the Los Angeles Antiquarian Book Fair being held this weekend at the Pasadena Convention Center. "The collection is the best in the world and its rare quality will attract a lot of attention," she added.

Margaret stared at the article with a little dismay. She knew she had been slightly misquoted, and the context of her comments had been changed, which she would try to explain to everyone. However, she also knew that she did basically agree with the gist of the article, as did probably everyone else who was thinking about the auction. It was just that no one else had been so forthright in public comments; their world was generally one of caution and reticence.

Simon Katz just nodded when he saw her. He understood.

A couple of other dealers, in good humor, said things like, "Hi, Margaret; are you saving up your pennies?" and "I guess I'll be wasting my time to go to the auction now."

Margaret just shrugged and smiled.

Louis Wing was back at the fair and he approached Margaret.

"Well, I guess the game is on," he said.

"Don't kid yourself, Louis, the game has been on ever since the auction was announced. The article just said what everyone knows, even if I didn't actually say it. You were there; you heard the interview."

"I know. I also know you are right. We need to talk about our strategy for the sale sometime soon."

"Of course," said Margaret with a slight twinge. Louis was obviously presuming her close involvement with him at the sale. That was fine in a way, as Louis was a big collector and he would undoubtedly participate seriously, but she wasn't sure she wanted the relationship to be an exclusive one. There were a lot of books involved and there would be a lot of action.

Hadrian Wall walked by at that moment, accompanied by his fellow Vancouverite Chester Chalk.

"There's some of our big competition, Cheese," he whispered.

"To be sure, Stone. But don't worry about that; it's not that we won't have lots of competition."

"Right. What does he have over us except an extra billion dollars?"

"We will just need to focus on what really matters to us and concentrate on that. We can't get distracted by what others do."

"I know. That's why I need you as my advisor."

Louis and Margaret; Hadrian and Chester; perhaps Jeremy and Alan; Simon; many others. It had started.

10

Herb Trawets looked across the expanse of booths. He hadn't come to the fair for the first two days, but he was here Sunday morning. He now lived a few hours up the California coast and he couldn't stay away. This had been his world for many decades.

Herb, whose real name was Yrrab, had owned an antiquarian bookstore, Herb's Books, in Seattle for a long time. He had been reasonably successful and was well respected in the industry. He had sold his business and retired from active involvement a couple of years ago.

Herb's unique identity was that he had been the main supplier of books and advice about antiquarian collecting to Ray Cartwright, the Seattle-based businessman who was now the President of the United States. The relationship had been very active up through Cartwright's tenure as Vice President. Although Herb kept a lookout for specific books that might be of interest for Cartwright's collection, the President's interest had been quite dormant since his election.

There was one other thing. Herb was a swindler, but no one else knew that.

Herb did wonder if there would be anything in the Cushing auction that would entice the President to bid. He would screen the list carefully when it was published. He certainly knew the President's collection well and what might be of interest.

He had smiled when he saw the newspaper article yesterday. The Cushing auction was going to be the Streeter sale all over again, probably with even more action. Although no one was going to be caught by surprise the way they were last time, he thought.

He worked his way up and down the aisles, greeting many people. He didn't dwell on the books, but he certainly scanned the shelves and noticed the prices being asked for volumes with which he was familiar. It appeared that prices had firmed up a bit over the past year.

He spent quite a while talking to Margaret Thomas. He had known her father, Thaddeus Thomas, very well, and he almost felt like an uncle to her. They discussed the general state of the business and borderline gossiped about other dealers. Of course, he mentioned the newspaper article, and he agreed with her that the reporter's story was pretty well on the mark.

When Margaret mentioned that she had essentially been misquoted, Herb laughed and said, "I expect that the reporter gathered his perspective about the Cushing auction from talking to many people, and then he just combined it all into a simpler description by attributing it to you. It doesn't really matter; there was nothing in the story that everyone didn't already know."

"You are probably right," she conceded.

"I don't know that I will be involved. My time has passed."

Margaret looked at him and winked. "Unless you have an interested customer, of course."

He shrugged, but in his private thoughts he hoped she was right.

Herb had pleasant conversations with Simon Katz and Jeremy Boucher before he encountered Colin Mackenzie, one of the largest dealers in London. They were good friends who had collaborated on many book deals over the years.

"Hello, Yrrab. It's great to see you here. How is retirement in the California sun?" Colin always used Herb's proper name; it was a British thing, Herb surmised.

"Hello, Colin. Life is good, although at times like today I miss the action a little. How are things with you?"

"Also fine. Our market has settled down a bit now with the quieter political and financial environments."

"That's good."

"Are you staying over in L.A.? Perhaps we could catch dinner, or at least a pint? I will be heading back home tomorrow but I could meet you later today. The fair will be over by five o'clock and it will take me a couple of hours to pack up, or at least do what I need to before I delegate the mundane details. I could meet you in the lounge in the hotel next door about seven thirty."

"I'd like to do that."

"Superb. I will meet you there."

As Herb was heading in the general direction of the exit, he saw Alan Page walking towards him.

Tensing up slightly, he greeted him casually. "Hi, Alan."

Encountering Alan was always awkward for Herb.

Alan had been the innocent, somewhat naïve go-between in the complex scam that Herb had pulled off a couple of years ago. He had managed to sell a completely fake document attributed to Francis Drake to Ray Cartwright for a total cost of $2.5 million. After the disbursements to Alan, Herb had pocketed $2.3 million, less some handling fees, and had even collected another $200,000 for helping Ray raise the money through an elaborate money-laundering scheme. No one knew that Herb was even involved. He had remained invisible and he didn't believe they could ever track him down, even if the President ever learned that the document was a fake.

Nevertheless, he was, as always, a little nervous when he talked to Alan. What if he finally recognized Herb's voice as the one he had heard on the phone many times as Frank Drake, the supplier of the Sir Francis Drake document?

For Alan, encountering Herb was always fun; he had always admired him. He knew that Herb had somehow been involved with Ray Cartwright's raising of the money to buy the Drake document when it seemed impossible to arrange. He also knew that that initiative had involved Simon Katz somehow, but he hadn't figured that part out. He was sure that Herb had no idea about Alan's involvement with the Drake deal. In fact, he wasn't even sure that Herb knew about the Drake connection at all, since he didn't know how much information Ray Cartwright had shared.

"Hi, Herb. Good to see you. Have you been checking out all the booths and dealers? I'm sure you must know everyone here."

"Not quite. Just catching up on friends and the news."

"Me too," replied Alan. "We both used to have booths at this event. You retired and I was just driven away by the competition," he continued. It was said easily, since it was true and they both knew it. If anything, Alan was very realistic and very comfortable with his role in the rare book world.

"Yes, I retired, but I know you just moved on to other ventures. I'm sure you are as busy as ever."

"That's true, I must admit."

"Are you still traveling a lot?"

"Yes. I seem to be spending more and more time in China and Russia. I'm convinced there are huge opportunities there, but the cultures are so different. There are no established open markets, bureaucracy is intense, and they are determined to protect anything to do with their heritage. I can't just go in and buy a rare book and haul it home."

Herb smiled. This uncharacteristic sharing by Alan actually enhanced his impression of him. Alan was a deeper thinker than he realized. Since Herb had a Persian heritage, and was well aware of dealings and manipulations with international jurisdictions, he understood what Alan was saying. Of course, Alan didn't know any of that. Herb Trawets from Seattle was a very different persona from Yrrab Enaed Trawets, whose father came from Iran via Great Britain.

11

At seven thirty that evening, Herb Trawets was seated in a comfortable, padded booth along the back wall of the lounge in the Pasadena Convention Center Hotel. Being Sunday evening, the place was relatively quiet, but there were some people he recognized from the book fair at various tables. He knew they were all letting down a bit after three busy days and, for many of them, a long day of travel ahead.

That certainly applied to Colin Mackenzie who appeared right on the minute. Herb thought that was not a coincidence. He was like Phileas Fogg, arriving back at the Reform Club in London in 1872 after taking exactly eighty days to circumnavigate the world.

"Over here," Herb quietly called out with a wave of his hand.

"Right, Yrrab."

As Colin sat down, a waitress came over and they ordered drinks, a red wine for Herb and a gin martini for Colin.

"That will taste good after three busy days," continued Colin.

Any of the other dealers in the lounge who noticed Colin and Herb would all have the same impression: "There are two of the stalwarts of the industry."

Colin Mackenzie was definitely the more renowned of the two, being a leading London dealer and world-wide expert. His neat white hair, carefully trimmed moustache, and impeccable suit all defined his persona, as did his formal, precise grammar. Everyone knew that Colin was a very shrewd businessman.

Herb Trawets was almost a grandfather figure to many of the American dealers. Now nearing 70 and retired, he was always polite and had always been available to talk or deal, again in a quiet, reserved way.

"Was it worth the long trip over here?" Herb asked Colin.

"Certainly, it always is. Even in slow years it's worthwhile, just for the opportunity to maintain contacts and to establish new ones. It also helps me get a pulse on what's happening in the American market. It can be quite different than in Britain."

"Things are fine?"

"Last year was good for sales."

"That's good to hear. Any sense of why things have picked up?"

"I think it's just the economy and growing confidence by the buyers. I couldn't detect anything else."

"What about the coming Cushing sale? Has it had an effect?"

"No, I don't think so. Although some major dealers may have started thinking about it and there was the article in the newspaper on Saturday, I don't believe that many people are really that aware of it. The catalogue of the collection hasn't been issued and the date of the sale hasn't been set yet."

"You are probably right. Those of us who are close to the market for key antiquarian travel and exploration books probably overestimate the awareness of others."

"Actually, Yrrab, that is precisely why I was pleased to see you here and why I am glad we could get together now."

"Oh?" replied Herb, a little surprised; he had assumed they would just be sharing a casual time, probably reminiscing.

"Yes, on the long flight over here from London, I was thinking about what opportunities the Cushing auction might create. When I saw you, the ideas gelled.

"I am sure you, and a lot of other people in the business, are wondering if this sale might be a repeat of the Streeter phenomenon. If so, prices for everything in the travel and exploration category will then jump up. This means people will start holding books out of the market and try to buy books at today's prices. It's a matter of who does it, how they do it, and when they do it.

"We know most of the large players in the business and how they do business. They will certainly start holding some important books back and may become more aggressive at regional book fairs and routine auctions.

"I am thinking that there is a large under-market of book dealers who are legitimate dealers in quality books, but who are not specialists in this area. They probably don't go to many book fairs outside their own region. Many of them are limited users of the internet search and sales sites. Collectively, they probably have a lot of books of interest, since collectors relocate, families move on, and books do drift back into book dealers' possession. You know: estate sales, family breakups, financial needs. It happens every day.

"Well what if we could tap into that source?"

At this point Herb interjected, "Won't others be doing the same thing?"

"Maybe, to a point, but we would have a big advantage."

After a pause, Herb took the bait. "What's that?"

"Money, knowledge, and the time to do it on a large scale."

Herb just looked back at Colin with a puzzled look.

Colin continued, "There are still seven to nine months until the sale; I think everyone expects it to be held after summer, sometime after your Labor Day and before Christmas. We should think of American

Thanksgiving as a target. That's a long way off in the everyday business cycle. I suspect others will wait before doing much. That creates the time we need.

"We have unrivaled knowledge of this general market niche, and you, in particular, have an amazing understanding and network in the U.S.

"And, if you are willing, being retired, you have the time to pursue these ideas. Who else can? Certainly no one else with your knowledge has it. The big players are too busy; the junior book scouts don't have the knowledge."

"Is it likely to be worth the effort?"

"That is where my doodling on the flight comes in.

"What if we assume there are a few reputable booksellers in each reasonably-sized city in America and that each one has accumulated some books of interest? If you could visit twenty-five or thirty cities over the next three months, find three to six good bookstores in each one, and on average find just a few books in each one of those, it would work."

"You're obviously way ahead of me with that analysis. Do those assumptions actually create a worthwhile opportunity?"

"Assume you visit five booksellers in thirty cities; that would be 150 stores. That would likely involve six or seven one-week trips to various regions. Then, assume you find five books of interest on average; that's 750 books. The individual sites would vary significantly, but I think that's a cautious estimate.

"I estimated a distribution of 300 books with an average retail value of $500; 300 with a value of $1,000; 100 at $3,000; and 50 at $5,000. That would be a total value of $1 million. That's likely low since I expect you will find a few very valuable books.

"Assuming you can buy them at an average 25 percent discount, we could resell them at a $250,000 profit, even if the market doesn't change. I could do that over a year or so at the normal book fairs and auctions in the U.K. Thus, there is little downside risk.

"On the upside, if the Cushing sale does stimulate the market another 25 percent, we make another $250,000. There is even more upside potential."

"You'd be willing to put up $750,000 to do that?"

"Yes. Actually more. I expect you would find more opportunities than I calculated. I also suggest that you could work your network of acquaintances in the mid-sized bookshops, those who do go to regional book fairs, such as Seattle and Sacramento, and buy an equal volume of books. Perhaps the discount would only be 15 or 20 percent, but the values could be higher."

"That's a lot of money."

"I can provide as much as $3 million in total."

Another long pause.

"How would our arrangement work?" Herb asked, almost in a whisper.

"For your time, expertise, and contacts I would give you 25 percent of the profits we realize. Worst case, for you, that would likely be $50,000 to $75,000. The upside? Twice that? Who knows? $250,000? $500,000?"

Herb was a bit stunned. This was a lot to absorb immediately.

"Colin, that is fascinating and enticing," he said candidly. "I just need a little time to think it through."

"That's understandable. I will still be here in the morning if you want to have breakfast together. We can certainly keep in contact by telephone and with e-mail."

With that, Colin flagged down the waitress and ordered another martini—Beefeater gin, of course.

"Another wine, Yrrab?"

"Make it two martinis."

Herb's mind was reeling with all the ramifications of Colin Mackenzie's proposal when he headed back to his hotel room, after they had finished their drinks and consumed a lounge-menu dinner.

He was excited about the proposal. He was a bit bored in his retirement, and this would give him something to focus on with the possibility of a relatively decent payoff. He had to admit that his retirement nest egg wasn't as financially comfortable as he had assumed, given the real estate pressures and investment market softness of the recent past. Privately, he was sure hoping that President Cartwright's new regime was going to continue to improve that.

His ego admitted that he liked the idea of being a participant in the business with the Cushing auction looming. His self-imposed invisibility would end for a while.

Pouring himself another glass of wine from the minibar in his room, he thought through the numerics that Colin had presented in their discussion. He was sure that the opportunities would be there; it would just be a matter of finding them, which would require research, networking, and travel. That was easy.

He even started to create his cover story, as if he needed one. He would just be taking advantage of his retirement and heading out to see America. Naturally, he would seek out bookstores and booksellers wherever he went; that was in his blood. Picking up a few books here and there would be second nature. He would not be sending out any market signals to others.

By the time he went to bed he knew that his answer to Colin in the morning would be yes.

12

It was a sunny April day in New York. The New York Antiquarian Book Fair was underway at the Park Avenue Armory on the upper east side of Manhattan, near 67th Street.

Although very similar to the February California fair in structure and layout, the mix of dealers and the range of books were quite different. There was a much greater preponderance of literature, sociology, science, and philosophy, although there were still many dealers who dealt in travel and voyages of exploration.

Simon Katz was looking over the crowd and he was pleased with the attendance and the activity he had seen so far. He brought a somewhat different selection of books here; generally a more expensive level. His books in California might have averaged $10,000 to $20,000 whereas the average here was closer to $50,000. He had many more books here in the $100,000 to $500,000 range.

A casual observer would assume that the difference reflected a more affluent customer base at this fair. That was somewhat true, but it wasn't the whole story. For California, he had to transport many boxes of heavy books across the continent, and so he took a selection that he hoped would lead to many sales. His business was located in New York, and so his display at the New York book fair was more designed to establish his reputation as a truly upscale dealer. Any customer at the fair could also very easily go to his shop in midtown Manhattan to see his full inventory of books. In fact, that was an ideal outcome for him with any new customers he met here. Once they started to deal with Simon, they inevitably developed a good relationship and would deal with him long term.

The book market had been relatively stable for the past year. Sales had been steady and he had been able to source good books on his various trips to Europe and regional book fairs in places such as San Francisco, Seattle, and Toronto. Unsolicited book offers also came in steadily from individuals and family estates, given his reputation.

He hadn't thought much about the Cushing collection since the sale was first announced. There really wasn't much to do until the details emerged, and he knew very well that the cataloguing and creation of detailed descriptions for a major collection took a lot of work. The final auction catalogue would list each book separately, with a glossy photo and text describing the book's contents, its place in history, its ownership provenance, its condition and completeness, and any other special features about it.

He had heard rumors that the catalogue would be issued around Labor Day and that the sale would be in late October, but that had not been confirmed.

He hadn't detected any impact on the current market from the pending sale.

During the fair he had chatted with Jeremy Boucher, Margaret Thomas, Graham Maltsby, Colin Mackenzie, and many others, but those conversations had been very general. He had even run into Herb Trawets, a bit of a surprise, since he thought Herb had retired.

There had been one customer interaction in his booth this afternoon that was slightly unusual. Two Asian men had walked in, looked over the titles of his books in silence, picked one four-volume set out, and looked at it in detail in what seemed to be an inspection of its quality. Then, after a nod between them and a brief comment by the older one in some foreign language, the younger of the two stepped over to him, pulled out a Hong Kong bank Visa card, and said, "We'll take these books, please."

In New York it certainly wasn't unusual to encounter Chinese individuals, even ones who appeared to be visitors rather than Americans by their dress and their language usage. What was unusual was that neither of them had commented on his books, asked any questions, or even tried to negotiate a lower price.

They had purchased a copy of Du Halde's 1735 publication about the history and geography of China. It was a compilation of the journals of twenty-seven different Jesuit priests who had travelled in China, written in French, and contained dozens of maps and illustrations. What makes the book of interest to collectors of maritime exploration books is that this publication also contains the first European report of Bering's 1728 voyage in the north Pacific between Siberia and Alaska. One of its maps was the very first to show parts of today's Alaska.

The set sold for $50,000. Simon reflected that an established customer, or even a promising new one, could have had it for $45,000 or less.

13

Herb Trawets and Colin Mackenzie had dinner together again. Herb was updating Colin on the details of his activities over the previous two months.

"Colin, I have had a busy time pursuing our plan. Since we met in February, I've been carefully scanning and selectively buying books from my network of dealers in the Pacific Northwest, and I've made four one-week trips to various regions to visit antiquarian book shops.

"Each trip covered four different cities. I made two trips to the Midwest, one to Texas, and one to the Southwest. I covered cities like Chicago, Detroit, Cleveland, Cincinnati, Milwaukee, Minneapolis, St. Louis, Houston, Dallas, and Phoenix. There are still many areas to cover, notably the eastern states. Next week, after this fair, I will visit upstate New York and New England. Soon I will travel to Pennsylvania, Virginia, the Carolinas, and Florida. The list just keeps expanding.

"As we knew, there are only a small number of quality booksellers in each city, even the larger ones. However, the number of books of interest I found in each one was more than I expected, usually five to ten per store. I found myself needing to enforce a discipline around the quality of the books, since some of the books were in less than great shape—perhaps a reason they have drifted to the secondary markets and hadn't sold at regional book fairs. However, there were still many books of interest.

"Very few of the dealers I met knew me, but my knowledge and interest in the books always caught their attention, and my story of being a travelling retiree made sense to them. Thus, it was quite easy to get a reasonable discount off their asking prices, which in many cases were already lower than the markets we work in.

"The most significant item I found was a set of George Vancouver's journals that were published in 1798, complete with the folio of maps and illustrations. The contents were complete and in very good condition. However, the bindings were in quite bad shape; one of the front covers was almost detached. I guess that was why the set was sitting in a bookstore in San Antonio without attracting attention. We know that such a set can be completely rebound with quality materials, in the style of the period, for a few thousand dollars. I purchased the set for $20,000. Once repaired, even at today's market prices, we can resell the set for at least three times that, probably more.

"There was another opportunity area that also surfaced in many of the stores. As we know, many books have been broken up over the centuries and their maps and illustrations have been sold and collected separately. They make colorful and interesting wall hangings and decorator pieces. It's always a great shame if complete books in good shape are broken up for that purpose, but over time many books do deteriorate and thus a salvage operation is worthwhile. Well, many of the bookstores have maps and illustrations displayed on their walls. Although they are for sale, I got the impression that, in many cases, they have just become part of the décor and haven't been given much thought or attention; they look like they have been hanging there a long time.

"There were quite a few of those that fit our areas of interest, and often the prices attached to them are quite out of date. That is, they're very low. I've found a couple of dozen great specimens already.

"Colin, with another half-dozen trips over the next few months, I'll have no difficulty reaching the $3 million target for quality merchandise."

"That's great news, Yrrab. It seems our initiative is working just fine. I don't detect any unusual action in the market. This week's New York fair has shown stable prices. Our success will truly be due to your having the time and expertise to pursue the books. Most dealers could not find the time to do such a thing."

14

Louis Wing had just finished his traverse of the booths at the New York fair. He was a little disappointed, but not surprised. He was in New York for business and had decided to drop by.

Simply put, he had amassed a very elaborate collection in his area of interest, and it was difficult to find anything here that made the trip worthwhile. Dealers tended to bring items that would have wider appeal and he already had most of them. Besides, he received the periodic catalogues of new acquisitions from most of the larger dealers, and he often received direct e-mails from them if they found something they thought would be of particular interest to him; he was a well-known collector in their world.

On top of that, Margaret Thomas was always scanning the book universe for him. Although she was younger than Louis, she acted as a bit of a mother hen towards him, bordering on being possessive, and perhaps jealous, when he dealt with others. This relationship did help him find desirable books early in their market appearance, but it also made things a bit awkward when others were involved.

He recalled a time at the California fair a couple of years earlier when he had purchased a book of interest from Simon Katz; it was a mid-range book worth about $10,000. When he told her about it, since he always kept her informed of what was in his collection, she became quite miffed.

"I have that book in my inventory," she said. "Why didn't you ask me?"

"Well, I guess I assumed that if you had a book that would be of interest to me, you would have already offered it to me. Besides, it seemed like a good deal," he said a bit aggressively.

"We have been focusing on other items lately; I just hadn't got to it," she replied somewhat defensively.

They had just left it at that.

He decided to head back to Margaret's booth before he left the fair. Today she was dressed in bright pink.

"Hi again, Margaret. I am heading out now and will be flying back to California in the morning."

"It was good to see you here. Did you find anything of interest?"

"No, nothing caught my eye."

"Have a good trip. I'll see you back in California."

"By the way, have you had any more thoughts about the Cushing sale?"

"Not really. I don't know what we can do about a bidding strategy until we see the actual list of books. We know that Reggie had a great collection; we just don't know the details. Therefore, we don't know which books you will be particularly interested in. It seems the catalogue is still three or four months away."

"OK. I just want to be sure we get very focused on the key items."

As he walked away, she was thinking that she had to be careful in dealing with Louis. She definitely wanted to work with him, but she also expected that she would be interested in more items than Louis would be.

Simultaneously, he was thinking that perhaps he needed to involve someone else, as well as Margaret, in planning his auction strategy. It was always better to have more than one opinion.

Just then he saw Herb Trawets walking towards the exit. "There's an idea," he thought. "Herb's an expert and retired; maybe he could help me?" Then he reflected further: "I wonder what he is doing here? Perhaps he still scouts out books for Ray Cartwright. Ray would certainly be a formidable opponent in a bidding war if it came to that. I guess I'll wait that idea out for a while."

15

On September 3rd, the day after Labor Day, a simple notice appeared in the *New York Times* and the *Los Angeles Times*, placed by BB Bookshelf Auctions. It was a major international auction house, headquartered in New York, which specialized in books and paintings. It was a relatively new organization, having been created by Barnaby Barkley less than a hundred years ago, just after the Second World War. After all, Christie's and Sotheby's started in the mid-1700s, and Bonhams and Waddingtons started in the mid-1800s.

"An auction of rare books from the collection of the late Mr. Reginald Cushing will occur on October 29 and 30 in our New York main auction hall. The listing of items for sale and more information can be found on our website: www.auctionbbbny.com"

It was a minor placement, but it certainly caught the attention of people in the know. When they saw the announcement, they all immediately searched for more information.

On the site was a more elaborate form of the announcement with times, addresses, and instructions for registering. It said that a complete catalogue of the items for sale would be available on October 1. Finally, it had a brief description of each of the books to be sold—almost four hundred of them.

Every person who visited the website had a similar reaction. Margaret Thomas probably expressed the feelings most graphically.

"Damn it! It's just a teaser! That Cushing family is working this sale for all it's worth. Can you imagine a list of important books like that having just the titles and short summaries of their content? At the least, there should be some indication of condition and any special features or provenance. This is like a menu at a fancy restaurant listing 'beef, chicken, pork and fish: take your choice.' What a waste of time." A few more expletives followed.

Booksellers such as Simon Katz, Jeremy Boucher, Graham Maltsby, and Stuart Scott just shrugged and waited for the next step.

Collectors such as Louis Wing and Hadrian Wall looked at the list with a bit more focus and circled items that might be of interest to them, depending on the details.

Colin Mackenzie and Herb Trawets compared the list to the books they had accumulated over the previous six months and decided they had covered the genre quite well.

Herb also decided it was time to contact Ray Cartwright.

16

Herb had been involved with Ray Cartwright for over twenty years, teaching him about the antiquarian book business and advising him on his collection. He had sourced and sold many books to him over the years.

Since Ray Cartwright had been elected President of the United States they had not had much contact. Obviously, he was occupied with more important things and his book collecting had been relegated to the back burner.

Once in a while, since even in retirement Herb kept his antennae out, he would identify a book that he thought the President would like to add to his collection. Then he would contact Ray's executive assistant, Elsie Browning, who he had dealt with for many years, and provide her with a summary of the book. Usually, without any other information, he would hear back that Ray would like the book and that his personal administrator, Maria Rodriguez, would be in touch for the payment and delivery details. Ray Cartwright needed to keep his personal financial dealings separate from his official activities. Herb knew that only too well from the big book deal of a few years ago.

In this case, he needed some more general instructions from the President. Did he want to become involved in the Cushing auction or not? There were certainly some books on the list that should be of interest to Ray.

He called Elsie Browning and, after giving her a general outline of what was happening, he agreed to send her a two-page description of the auction. He presumed that everything in the President's world was boiled down to two pages.

Herb had Colin's agreement that he could work with others on the Cushing auction. Colin presumed it would include Ray Cartwright. Colin didn't need Herb's involvement if he was going to be bidding for himself or for other customers; Herb would just create another unnecessary complication. They did not have any conflict, since their book accumulation effort was now complete and that endeavor was not directly related to the auction.

About a week after sending out the summary of the Cushing sale, Herb received a call from Elsie.

""Hello, Mr. Trawets. The President would like to discuss the book sale with you. He will be back home in Seattle next weekend; would that be a convenient time for you to meet him, say 2:00 p.m. on Saturday?"

"That would be fine," replied Herb.

He had noted two things in the call from Elsie. First, her tone had become much more formal. He guessed that was inevitable when you were calling for the President of the United States, even to an old acquaintance. Second, she had forgotten, or perhaps didn't care, that he no longer lived in Seattle.

Over the next few days Herb tried to compile a list of the items he thought the President might be interested in. He had the simple auction list and the list of Ray's holdings, which he was privy to based on their long term relationship. Of course, the list did not include the Sir Francis Drake document.

He ended up with four books.

The following weekend he took the short flight up to Seattle and he headed over to Ray Cartwright's home.

He had been there before, but not since Ray had become President. The presence of security people and the need to check in and be vetted by a cadre of people was certainly much more intense than when Ray had just been the Vice President.

Ray had a nice residence: a large, traditional-style, two-story structure with a separate garage and guest house, on a somewhat secluded small acreage, with a view through the trees of Puget Sound. Herb assumed that the neighbors were not pleased with the disruptions, even if they were proud that the President was from there.

"Hello, Herb. Welcome," greeted Ray Cartwright.

"Hello, Mr. President," replied Herb.

"How are you doing?"

"Just fine, thank you. You are certainly busy, sir. Thank you for seeing me."

"Quite the contrary, Herb. Of course I'm busy; it comes with the job. Thanks for keeping in touch. I don't have much time to think about my book collection these days. I'm glad you're thinking about it, even in your retirement. We do go back a long way."

After a few more general greetings, Ray brought the subject around to the book auction and asked Herb a number of questions about the collection in general and the auction process itself. Then he asked the key question.

"Herb, do you think there is anything in the sale that I should be especially interested in?'

"Well, sir, it will really depend on the details that we haven't seen yet. I have identified a few books that would be good additions to your collection. They might be found elsewhere from time to time, I'm sure, but I expect the Cushing copies will have some special significance.

"Also, there may be something distinctive about the Cushing copies of things you already own. You could upgrade."

They discussed the various books for quite a while.

"In reality, Herb, I haven't placed a lot of value on the special provenance of specific copies of a publication. It's the explorer and his story that intrigues me, not whether or not someone else in particular has owned my specific copy. There will be exceptions, of course, but generally that's my position."

"I understand."

"Do you expect the auction will be a lively one?"

"I expect so, especially for exceptional items, such as those ones having some unique provenance. There has been quite a bit of anticipation around this sale."

"Herb, after going through all this material, I think I will take a pass on this sale. I'm not sure it's good politics for me to be bidding large amounts of money in a public book sale. Sure, people know that I am wealthy, but we need to somehow not flaunt that."

"You know I could do the bidding for you. You wouldn't need to be personally involved."

"There are no secrets in politics, Herb. No, I'll pass unless something extraordinary turns up when you see the details."

"That's fine, sir."

"Thanks for coming up here and spending this time with me. It's been great to see you again."

After Herb had left, Ray Cartwright mulled over what he had heard. He hadn't paid much attention to his book collection since becoming President. However, when he was home like this, he did sometimes browse through various volumes for relaxation.

At those times, he would often extract the Sir Francis Drake document that he had secretly purchased a few years ago from its locked cabinet and admire it. As he had told Herb, he wasn't particularly enamored with some special provenance of a specific volume of a book, but this was different. It was one-of-a-kind. It was so special that no one even knew it existed.

Of course, Herb didn't know anything about this document. Even though Herb had helped him raise the funds for buying it, and had been involved in the money transfer to pay for it, he didn't know what the document actually was.

Over the past few years, Ray had done some thinking about the Drake document and what he would eventually do with it.

In seven or eight years, sometime after his Presidency was finished, he would be receiving the extensive de Bry collection that he had bought from the Armstrong family in Boston on a deferred basis. That collection was now on loan to Harvard University.

Perhaps then he would extend the loan of the de Bry collection to Harvard and add on the Drake document. Ten years after his initial purchase should be long enough to keep it secret. He knew that the sellers wanted him to keep it secret forever, but that wasn't going to happen. The true story of Drake's exploration of the Pacific Northwest should be known. Consigning it to a place like Harvard might preclude other claims and expectations for it.

"Herb will be surprised when he learns about the Drake document," Ray mused. "I hope he is still in good enough health to fully appreciate it when it emerges from secrecy."

As Herb exited the President's home, he couldn't help thinking, "I sure hope Ray Cartwright never learns that his secret Sir Francis Drake document is a fraud—at least not while I'm still around."

17

October 1st. The auction catalogue was finally released.

It looked remarkably similar to the catalogue that had been issued for the Streeter sale years earlier. It was in two volumes with linen-cloth hard covers. Each of the almost four hundred books was described in detail with accompanying photographs. Some book descriptions took up four pages. The only noticeable difference was that the catalogues were dark blue rather than green.

There were only three thousand copies printed. Yes, it was much anticipated and coveted in the antiquarian book world dedicated to voyages of exploration, but that was a limited market. The catalogue itself would become a collector's item, with its rich descriptions of important volumes.

The sale was to be held in four weeks' time over two days, October 29th and 30th, with each session starting at 2:00 p.m. New York time. This was a convenient time, since it would be 11:00 a.m. in Los Angeles, 7:00 p.m. in London and 6:00 a.m. in Sydney. That was as good a balance as possible to accommodate bidders who may be linked in to the sale by phone or messaging.

The books would be available for inspection at the auction house for seven days before the actual sale.

The two volumes of the catalogue represented the sales list for each of the two days. With the normal brisk pace of such auctions, selling two hundred or so books in each session would take about four hours.

The Cushing collection was similar in content to the Streeter collection in that, although it covered general exploration such as early voyages around the world, it focused on the exploration of northwest North America, whether overland, up the Pacific coast, or across the Arctic.

The organizers of the auction could have divided the collection into subclasses to accommodate specific collectors, but they had decided to list all of the books alphabetically, as had been done for the Streeter sale. This had a number of advantages from the seller's point of view.

First, if any specific area generated high interest, and thus higher-than-expected prices, it would likely influence the action on the other interspersed subjects.

Second, for bidders who were focused on one category, it provided a bit more thinking time between items of interest. Again, this could provide time for bidders to consider higher-than-planned bids if the action was lively.

Third, it might entice some of the major players to engage in some joint bidding strategies to increase their chance of success, which again could lead to more determined bidding and higher prices.

Of course, that was all conjecture, but it didn't seem to have any downside risk for the seller.

Hundreds of orders had been placed for the catalogue over the previous month, and the auction house had carefully arranged for courier delivery that same day to everyone who had ordered them, anywhere in the world.

For BB Bookshelf Auctions, creating competition was now the main task.

As potential buyers read through the volumes, everyone's reaction was similar: "What an amazing collection! Reginald Cushing totally outdid himself."

As described, all of the books were in excellent condition. Many of them were in their original board covers and in the untrimmed state that they would have left the publishers. Centuries ago, books were bought untrimmed and unbound, with the buyer then following up with a bookbinder to finish the job. Books that were in their original, untouched state were the rarest and, therefore, most coveted by collectors.

Perhaps as importantly, most of the books had some special aspect to them—perhaps being signed by the author or having been previously owned by someone famous. The ultimate combination was to have a book signed by the author, dedicating it to an important person.

Over the decades Reginald Cushing had obviously encountered these outstanding copies and had kept them in his personal collection, constantly upgrading over time. He had the foresight, even in the early days when money was tighter, to set aside the best of what he found. It was one thing to deal in expensive books and to manage margins, cash flows, and lines of credit to make it work; it was another thing to set aside books worth meaningful dollars. Of course, as time went on and he became successful, that was not a problem.

As was customary, the auction house had indicated the expected range of value for each book. This was always a tricky proposition and sometimes the estimates could be wildly off, as they were for the Streeter sale.

Current listings for similar books and recent auction records from the industry provided some guidance for them. They would certainly take into account the condition and any special provenance of the books, which, in this case, added value. They tried to be reasonable in their estimates but also to suggest some upside potential, again primarily serving the seller's interests.

For example, a book that had some market reference at $10,000 would be listed with an expected range of $10,000-$15,000. A 30 to 50 percent upside was not unusual in such catalogues.

When you added up their estimates for all the books, it came to an amazing $15-$20 million.

As Simon Katz said to his associates as they reviewed the catalogue, "They don't know what these books will sell for. Sure, there are other copies of every one of them in the world, but almost all of these have a unique dimension. If there was a Vegas line on the over/under, I would take 'over $20 million'.

"What will a collector pay for a one-of-a-kind? That's what we need to decide. How aggressive can we be?"

Simon knew that there would be many people scanning the lists, deciding which items they wanted to focus on, and then, with a bit of angst, deciding how much they were willing to pay.

Simon approached it differently. He was in the business for the long term and so any purchase had to make sense financially. He also knew that markets didn't simply evolve linearly; there were real discontinuities from time to time. He had made a lot of money from the Streeter sale, both from the books he bought and, more significantly, from the increased value of his inventory. Would the Cushing sale give him the same opportunity?

He meticulously examined the catalogue. He placed the various books in subcategories: general, technical, Pacific, Arctic, and so on. This was not to focus his interest, since he was interested in all of it.

It was, first of all, to try to guess the competition in each category, although he knew that was probably a waste of time. There were too many dealers worldwide involved in the business, and this sale would attract many big-time collectors. It's always difficult to bid against motivated collectors. After all, they are bidding at the retail level and he is bidding wholesale. Where the opportunity comes is when the market is changing, and the old retail price becomes the new wholesale price. Then the collector balks and he strikes. Streeter all over again!

The second reason was to create a detailed sequence for the sale. Because there were many subsets of interest in the offering, he wanted to get some early indication during the auction as to what was really happening. Obviously, if all the early prices were in line with the current market, or were jumping ahead of the estimates, that would give him a sense of what was happening overall. But if one category was behaving abnormally, perhaps due to a particular collector or dealer, he didn't want to be fooled into thinking that applied to the whole sale.

He doubted that many other dealers looked at the sale in such detail.

18

In Vancouver, Hadrian Wall was looking at the catalogue volumes with Chester Chalk.

"There are sure some great books here," he said.

"Indeed, Stone. What catches your attention?"

"I'm looking at it more from the point of view of what interests me, plus what am I likely to be willing to bid. We know there will be a lot of interest and that these quality books will attract big bids."

"I agree, but we don't know what others will bid. All we can decide is what you're willing to pay."

"I know, but if the market is moving, we need to be aware of that. I don't want to be blindly bidding prices up in some frenzy, but I also don't want to be left behind because I was too timid."

Chester laughed. "Welcome to the world of big-time auctions. You weren't involved in collecting when the Streeter auction occurred. You have pretty well always dealt one-on-one with dealers, whether with me or at some book fair. This is different. It's fast and it's uncontrolled. Only planning and discipline will help you."

"OK. Let's start with the Arctic-related books, since that has always been my primary interest. I already have many of the books being sold, perhaps not in quite the pristine condition these seem to be and not with any special provenance, but that doesn't matter so much to me. I am mostly interested in the content and the sense of history.

"There are a few books that would be nice additions to my collection and I would be willing to bid in the range indicated, but I wouldn't chase them. There will be other copies on the market from time to time. We can refine that list later.

"Something that does catch my attention is the two-volume set of Theodore Swaine Drage's journals covering the voyage through the Hudson Strait in 1746 and 1747, published in 1749."

"I agree. This is from a very early stage of Arctic exploration, and it follows on the books published by Dobbs and Middleton a few years earlier that hotly debated the possibility of a Northwest Passage. It was quite a controversy in the political, military, and scientific circles of the day. This voyage was significant, and I know the publication is quite rare. I haven't seen a copy in the market for years. The description of the set that's for sale indicates it's in fine shape, and I don't see any other special features. That means that even if the auction is active we might be able to compete. What did you have in mind?"

"The auction house estimate shows a range of $35,000 to $50,000. I would certainly be willing to bid at the upper level, perhaps a bit more."

"That would link to auction tactics. There are specific bidding rules, plus some ingrained habits by many dealers at auctions. For example, once a bid reaches the $50,000 level, the minimum incremental bid allowed is $5,000.

"In preparing for an auction, some bidders will presume that other people will be tempted to bid to the top of the indicated range. Therefore, they often give instructions to bid 'plus one.' That means they will bid one increment over the indicated maximum; this helps the situation where someone else has actually made that same maximum bid amount in the bidding cycle.

"In our example, if you have a $50,000 maximum in mind, you authorize a bid of $55,000 in the case where someone else actually makes the $50,000 bid."

"Then we should bid up by two bid increments, to $60,000, in case someone does that to us."

"That's your call. I think it's a good strategy, giving you a real opportunity, but avoiding getting in too deep. We will also have some knowledge of earlier bidding levels; the Drage will come up about midway into the first day's session."

"The other area that always interests me is the science of exploration. Do you know that the biggest problem for navigation until the late 1700s was the inability to determine longitude at sea?

"Latitude was easy. Observations of the position of the sun and stars in the sky, and reference to nautical charts that linked to the calendar, allowed sailors to know quite precisely where they were in a north-south sense.

"However, an east-west determination was much more difficult. That's because the Earth rotates on its axis every twenty-four hours. To know where you are, east or west of somewhere else, means you need to know what time it is at both places when an observation is made. You can know the time where you are pretty accurately by observing the peak noon sun and keeping short term time with hourglasses or some other simple instrument. But to keep an awareness of time somewhere else, say Greenwich in London, you need a clock set to London time. But, they didn't have good enough clocks in the 1700s.

"Moon observations were not accurate enough and mechanical devices were not good enough. Imagine trying to keep time over a period of years, on a ship bobbing across the oceans, with storms and great changes in temperature and humidity. An error of even one hour meant you were off target by one thousand miles.

"This was of the highest priority to the military. Navies had lost many ships, even fleets, due to navigation errors. The British government offered a huge prize for anyone who could solve the problem.

"Finally, in the mid-1700s, a clockmaker named John Harrison invented a clock that was accurate enough. He was awarded the prize, but not without many years of controversy and intrigue. Captain James Cook was actually the one who first credibly attested to the adequacy of Harrison's device.

"You can see here in the catalogue that some of Harrison's publications about the design of his clock are included in the collection. The price estimates for some of the most important ones range between $300,000 and $750,000, well out of my league.

"However, there is a collection of British government Acts of Parliament related to the stimulus and recognition of the solution to the longitude problem. There are twenty-six different published Acts in the package, covering over one hundred years from 1714 to 1829, which encompasses the reigns of Queen Anne and Kings George II, III, and IV. The estimated price is $50,000 to $70,000. I would like to take a run at that package as well. The historical context is so important."

"OK. Let's carry on and refine your longer list, to be sure we know your priorities."

19

In Toronto, Stuart Scott was seated in his bookstore office. His shop was located in an old, three-story former residence on Avenue Road in the trendy Yorkville shopping area. It was also near the University of Toronto and the Royal Ontario Museum, which was convenient for many of his customers.

Anyone entering his store for the first time was always overwhelmed by the chaos. Every room in the three stories, plus the basement, was filled with bookshelves from floor to ceiling, separated by narrow aisles. Books filled the shelves and then spilled over to piles on the floor and on top of any other available surface, such as windowsills and chairs. However, in the world of booksellers, such a set-up was not that unusual. How Stuart knew what was in his inventory, let alone how to locate it, was a mystery to everyone.

Stuart looked like an antiquarian bookseller, as one would be cast in a movie. He was in his late fifties, slightly less than six feet tall, slightly overweight, with a long salt-and-pepper beard and small wire-rimmed glasses.

He was scanning the Cushing catalogue and, as had Hadrian Wall, was concentrating on the books related to Arctic exploration. He made a separate list of them and then, beside each one, he placed the name of one or two collectors he dealt with who could be interested.

Staring at the combined lists, he knew that he would need to be very careful in how he approached the individual collectors; there were obvious conflicts. Some of them were his longer-term, more-established customers. Some of them had more interest in very high-end items such as those in the Cushing collection. Others placed less importance on a book's individual provenance. Some of them had more money than others or, at least, a greater willingness to spend it on books.

When he finished fine-tuning his lists, he had narrowed his contact plan to four collectors. He avoided creating severe conflicts because of his knowledge of what each one already had in his collection and their specific areas of highest interest. Two of the collectors were in Toronto, one in Ottawa, and one in Montreal.

He then made a series of phone calls. As Chester Chalk had done with Hadrian Wall, he started to develop a bidding strategy with each of the customers; they would refine their approach over the next couple of weeks as the customers became more familiar with the details of the books and thought about their willingness to bid.

In Sydney, Australia, Graham Maltsby did almost the same thing, although he focused on Pacific Ocean ventures, as they were the ones that would interest his customers.

In California, Louis Wing had just completed a long telephone conversation with Margaret Thomas. They had discussed the auction list and had identified many books of interest. Louis did place value on quality and uniqueness. Margaret agreed to compile a detailed analysis of the individual books' characteristics and their likely premium value, although they knew that would be difficult. It would really come down to how much Louis, or someone else, was willing to pay.

Jeremy Boucher, in Columbus, looked at the book list with a somewhat different bias. He knew that he would be unlikely to compete successfully with the dealers and high-value customers whose main focus was on voyages and exploration. That was a somewhat secondary area for him. However, there was some overlap with general Americana interests, and Jeremy believed that collectors of that ilk might put even more value on relevant items.

The item that most interested him was the 1814 set of first-edition journals of the Lewis and Clark expedition. Their 1804 to 1806 journey up the Missouri River and across the Rocky Mountains to connect with the Columbia River and reach the Pacific Ocean was legendary. It had been ordered by President Jefferson to solidify the United States' claim to the Louisiana Territory, recently acquired from France, which stretched from New Orleans to the wilds of today's Montana. Jefferson also wanted to establish the feasibility of overland travel to the Pacific and to lay claim to the Pacific Northwest, which at the time was claimed by Spain, Britain, and even Russia in different areas.

The two-volume set of journals, complete with all maps and drawings, was in immaculate shape. Most importantly, this set was one of the few that President Jefferson owned. It bore Jefferson's signature, as well as William Clark's; Meriwether Lewis had died before the journals were published.

A similar set had sold at the Streeter sale for $300,000. The estimate in the current catalogue was $300,000 to $450,000. Jeremy thought that was probably right, with the upside quite likely.

He decided to contact a book collector he knew well in St. Louis who was likely to be very interested and capable of competing in the auction. That level was certainly too high for Jeremy to consider bidding himself, although there were a few other items he would consider bidding on.

Herb Trawets looked through the listings with curiosity but, since Ray Cartwright had decided not to get involved, he didn't plan on any other actions. He was confident that his extensive book-buying venture with Colin Mackenzie would be profitable. He, obviously, was hoping for very high prices to occur at the auction.

20

Alan Page also looked through the Cushing catalogue in detail but he couldn't see any real opportunity for himself. He didn't have the resources to compete at the expected price levels, and he didn't have any obvious contacts who would want him to act as their general agent. He needed to find some specific opportunity.

Then, a week later, he was surprised to receive a phone call from someone named Mr. Wu. He explained that he was interested in the Cushing auction and that Alan had been recommended to him as someone who could provide some advice and service. They had agreed to meet in New York just ten days before the sale.

Alan was very pleased with the call; he had to believe that it was a result of his extensive international travels, including Asia in the past couple of years.

When they met, Mr. Wu was very direct with him.

"Mr. Page, you are well aware that the economy of China has been growing quickly for the past few decades, and that there is a much more open attitude to the international marketplace now. There are individuals of influence and wealth who are very interested in Chinese history and who have developed significant collections of artifacts.

"A relatively new area of interest for some of these people is to collect items that describe how the western world interacted with and viewed China in earlier times, all the way from Marco Polo in the thirteenth century to the maritime explorers who approached from the Pacific Ocean in the eighteenth century.

"Some of the items coming up in the Cushing auction are outstanding copies of books of interest to those collectors, who truly value quality and have the funds to buy them.

"I am what you would call a broker; I locate and acquire such things. We also believe that, at times, it is better to keep a low profile so as not to disturb the market too much. I have been buying books online and at some book fairs over the past year.

"However, this auction is going to be a very high profile event. Therefore, we would like you to do the bidding for us at the auction. We also would want your advice on the books, the competition, and bidding tactics. For that, we offer to pay you ten percent of the purchase prices of items we buy."

Alan was pleased.

"I accept your offer. However, aren't you concerned that I will have an incentive to bid too much since that would increase my payment?"

For the first time, Mr. Wu's face broke into a bit of a smile.

"You are very honest with that comment, Mr. Page. Thank you. But it will not be a problem, since you will only bid what it takes to buy any given book, and we will buy every book that we are interested in."

That comment did take Alan by surprise. Just bid until you win! Wow!

21

Starting on October 22nd, a week before the auction, the books were available for inspection.

Hundreds of books lay out on tables, arranged in aisles for viewing, filling a large display room, a normal practice for any auction house.

Attendance over the week was steady, as dealers, collectors, and curiosity-seekers all came through. Even for people who had no direct interest or the money for buying the books, it was an opportunity to see some rare volumes that they would seldom, or never, see otherwise.

The most meticulous inspection of the books was undertaken by various representatives of major universities and public collections. It was in their nature. The reputation of Reginald Cushing and the detailed descriptions provided in the catalogues by the auction house satisfied most of the serious dealers and collectors. Those who did actually attend were often doing it more as a matter of form and curiosity.

There were a few dealers who inspected the books and put out summaries on their websites. They hoped this would be seen as a useful service by others who were not in New York and who might be useful contacts later. They confirmed the catalogue descriptions, sometimes effusively.

Two days before the sale, Simon Katz viewed the books, although it was in a cursory way. His staff had examined every book in detail. Simon had sent someone every day, so as to scout out who else was there. That hadn't really told him much, since most of the people were either familiar and expected or completely unknown to them.

One member of his staff did remark that there were a couple of Chinese individuals who spent a long time examining some of the books. Their description matched the two people who had bought the Du Halde from him at the New York book fair in April.

Simon had chosen this day for a couple of other reasons. One was that he could chat with the staff of the auction house about the sale. They were naturally very discreet and never divulged any specifics about other people who had attended. However, they inevitably displayed a sense of the event, whether by body language or tone. Simon concluded that the staff was very optimistic about the sale and not just saying the normal marketing fluff.

The second reason was that he quite expected to see other major dealers that day. Some would be there for the same reason he was. Others would be there because they would have flown in from other places and this was the logical time for them to attend.

Therefore, he was not surprised to see Margaret Thomas.

"Hello again, Margaret. Have you found any flaws yet?" he joked.

"Sure. These books are too good; they must be fakes," she joked back. They both laughed.

"It's going to be an interesting couple of days," she continued.

"Definitely. There's a lot of anticipation. For us, it's just like the Super Bowl for football players."

"Well, I hope I don't get tackled when I make a big move," she deftly answered.

"Or penalized for illegal motion," Simon said, perhaps a bit too boldly.

Again they both laughed.

At that moment they noticed Colin Mackenzie entering the display area and waved to him.

"Welcome, Colin," they both said almost simultaneously.

"Hello," he replied. "I arrived last night and thought it was time to see these wonderful books."

"Absolutely," agreed Margaret.

"They probably look even better to you with the pound at $1.75," teased Simon.

Colin just smiled.

Across the room, Alan Page observed the three of them. "Well," he thought, "there are the big hitters. Perhaps I'll have a surprise or two for them."

22

As the dealers departed from the book showing, Margaret Thomas pondered her predicament. She hoped she had covered her bases adequately.

She had been working diligently with Louis Wing on his bidding strategy. Louis was interested in many of the books and he had ample funds. She had helped him identify which books were truly unique, say due to some special provenance, and which ones were capable of being found some other place as well. Obviously, in the first instance you had to bid as much as you could justify to yourself for the ownership. In the second instance you needed to be more prudent and not get totally carried away.

The problem came with the set of Lewis and Clark journals, the ones signed by President Jefferson and by the explorer William Clark.

Louis Wing wanted those books and so did another one of Margaret's good clients, George Archer, based in L.A.

Margaret had tried to avoid dealing with Archer regarding the auction, to prevent any conflict in her dealings with Louis. However, he had called her two weeks ago and asked her directly for some advice, since they had been on the lookout for a pristine Lewis and Clark set for two years, well before the Cushing collection was known to be for sale.

"Margaret, that set of Lewis and Clark looks perfect; it's what we have been looking for. Don't you agree?"

"Yes, the set looks good," she had replied cautiously.

"They have estimated it will sell for as much as $450,000. Do you think it will take that much?"

"It might, George, but that's a lot of money. The one in the Streeter sale went for just under $300,000. Also, we will be able to find an excellent set of the journals, albeit without the signatures, for much less."

"This set is very special. I want to give it a real shot. If bidding goes up by $25,000 increments at that level, I would be willing to go two levels over the top estimate, $500,000."

"That's a big step," she had replied, wishing that George hadn't given her that information.

"I know. Will you be at the actual auction? Will you make the bids for me, up to that level?"

"George, I can't do that myself," she had answered truthfully, if somewhat incompletely, as she explained she had many clients who would be involved with the sale and she couldn't make individual bids for him.

"However, I can arrange for an associate, John Miller, to handle the bids for you, and you can finalize the bid levels and tactics with him."

"OK, I guess I understand. Have him call me."

Then she had a similar exchange with Louis Wing a week later.

"I really want those Lewis and Clark journals," he said in the middle of one of their meetings.

"They are good, but be careful," she had replied.

"What does that mean?"

"Well, there are good quality Lewis and Clark sets out there to be found. William Clark did sign a number of them. The defining thing here is having Jefferson's signature as well. But remember, Jefferson's signature can be found on many things; he was President after all."

"Sure, but it's still a unique combination."

"Oh yes; it's just a question of how much is it really worth? Remember, a similar set sold for under $300,000 a few years ago."

"What do you suggest?"

"I think $350,000 or $400,000 would be plenty. More would be overpaying," she ventured, trying hard not to show any emotion. She actually believed that was a fair value, but she also knew that George Archer was going to bid more—too much in her opinion. That didn't change the fact that she was in an ethical bind; she was advising Louis to stop bidding short of what she knew was going to happen.

After a pause, Louis said, "Alright, let's go up to $400,000."

Margaret hoped she had a credible denial story for Louis after the sale.

What Margaret didn't know was that Louis Wing had taken some further action, independent of her, after that conversation. He had detected something fishy in Margaret's advice about the Lewis and Clark books.

He had called Herb Trawets, as he had contemplated six months earlier in New York. After ascertaining that Herb was available to talk about the Cushing auction without conflict, information that in itself was valuable, he asked Herb to come to meet with him in San Francisco. As Herb lived only a few hours away, he agreed.

"Herb, welcome. Thank you so much for coming up here to meet with me. I know it's a bit of a drive for you."

"It's a pleasure, Louis, and the trip was quite pleasant. October is a great time of year in California; you know that."

"I do. Would you like a drink?"

After pouring a couple of glasses of fine California red wine, Louis came right to the point.

"Herb, I need some help with a back-up plan at the Cushing auction next week. I will be very candid, but I must ask you to keep our conversation in complete confidence; it's a sensitive situation."

"Of course, Louis. As I said on the phone, I have no conflicts of interest with the sale."

"The Cushing collection is truly outstanding. The number of signed books is amazing. I didn't even know that some of the explorers had signed copies of their publications. When I finished looking at the catalogues, I half expected to see a James Cook signed journal of his third voyage, or a George Vancouver signed volume, or a Sir Francis Drake endorsed journal."

Herb laughed at that statement, although he swallowed a bit at the reference to Drake. Louis's statement was a litany of the inside jokes in the industry; all of those explorers had died before their journals were published.

"It will be no surprise to you to know that I am working closely with Margaret Thomas on the sale. In fact, she will be making many of my bids. For various reasons, I don't want to be seen making too many actual bids at the auction, even though people might suspect she is acting for me.

"We have agreed on almost everything, but there is one item that has me concerned. She may have a conflict. I don't know that as a fact, but her actions have confused me.

"The Lewis and Clark journals are so distinctive. I know you've read the description. The auction house estimate is $300,000 to $450,000. I just know the interest will be high and the competition could be aggressive. Margaret has advised me that $400,000 is plenty to reflect value, and that level of bid should be adequate. Of course, depending on the bidding cycle, she would be able to increase that by one bid increment to $425,000.

"I want you to be at the auction and to observe the bidding on the Lewis and Clark item. If the bidding stops at or below $400,000, or you see her bid successfully at $425,000, we will know Margaret was right and that we have won. If it goes higher, that means someone else is involved. I am willing to go higher, but I don't want to divulge that to Margaret. In that case, you can step in and bid more."

Herb had taken all of this in without comment. It gave him a remarkable insight into Louis Wing's thinking and business tactics.

"How much more?" he asked.

"I'm convinced this is a once-in-a-lifetime shot for me. The other known, similar sets are now all tied up in government and institutional holdings; they won't be coming on the public market. I will bid up to $600,000."

Herb was stunned.

Louis continued, "I will pay for all of your expenses to go to New York for the auction and will pay you a $50,000 fee for doing this."

"Agreed," said Herb. "It should be very interesting and entertaining."

Herb also recognized that Louis had cleverly hedged his bets. If Margaret buys the books for him, even with the payment to Herb, Louis would get them for much less than his maximum level. If Herb buys the books, his payment would just replace the payment that Margaret would have received; surely, she would be receiving a commission on all their successful bids. Louis had put himself in a no-lose position, or phrased more positively, a win-win position. That is, unless someone else was willing to bid more than $600,000.

23

Finally, it was auction day.

BB Bookshelf Auctions was well organized and determined to be punctual; there were people plugged in from around the world in many different time zones.

The room was laid out in typical auction format. At the front of the room was a podium for the auctioneer and a set of easels for displaying the relevant sale item. A large screen was behind the podium; images of the item would be shown there. There were electronic tote boards on each side of the screen. The auctioneer's values would always be stated in American dollars, but the converted value in other currencies would also be shown there. For this auction, that included Euros, British pounds, Canadian dollars, and Australian dollars, since those areas were expected to generate the most interest.

Along the side walls of the room were many small desks with telephones. They were each staffed by an employee of the auction house. They would be communicating with individuals from anywhere in the world who had arranged for this service. They would be connected when their items of interest were imminent, and then the staff member would place the bids as instructed during the auction of that item.

Cell phones were not permitted in the auction hall. Dealers bidding on behalf of others would need to have specific instructions in hand. Of course, as the auction would proceed over the two days, they would get a better sense of the competitive atmosphere and general price levels. They could step out of the room to call their clients if it seemed necessary to review bidding strategies.

By five minutes before sale time, essentially everyone present was seated. The room was full. There were perhaps three hundred people—dealers, collectors, and curiosity-seekers.

Many individuals had carefully staked out their places. Some wanted to be up front, either to see well or to be seen to be bidding for some reason. Others wanted to be near the back, so as to be less obvious to other bidders. Some people tried to position themselves to be able to see other specific people, but that was difficult in a large crowd that tended to sit randomly. However, it was possible if you were determined. For example, Herb Trawets managed to sit where he could observe Margaret

Thomas and still be in a very visible spot to be seen by others, which was part of his plan.

At precisely 2:00 p.m. the auctioneer, Gunther Shultz, strode up to the podium and, with a single strike of his gavel, brought the room to silence.

After welcoming everyone, he then spent many minutes summarizing the rules of the auction and referring everyone to the details as laid out in the catalogues. Well-run auctions seldom have problems, but, when a problem does occur, it can be very awkward, particularly if someone is mistaken in thinking they have the winning bid and doesn't keep bidding when the auctioneer closes out an item.

There were many staff members spread throughout the auction room to aid the process. They helped the auctioneer spot bids; they tried to keep everyone informed as to who had made the most recent bid; and they tried to urge on bids from anyone who had shown any interest in the item being offered.

"Ladies and Gentlemen, we have Lot Number One."

Gunther Shultz was a seasoned auctioneer. He even had a nickname among the clientele who frequently attended his auctions, "Gunfire."

His nickname didn't come from having a rapid-fire delivery or banter, such as the one you hear at a country livestock auction, or a local estate auction of furniture and artwork, or even those now-popular television shows about storage locker or pawn shop auctions. No, Gunther maintained a quiet, but steady pace as he politely said something like,

"I have a bid at 100; do I hear 110?"

Slight pause.

"Again 100, looking for 110."

Another pause.

"That's once . . . twice . . . sold."

It was only when you checked your watch and realized that he averaged about one minute per item, even involving large sums of money, that you understood his method. The message was simple: "Pay attention. Be decisive. Don't waste my time."

He and his auction house were going to collect twenty percent of the sales price, thus netting perhaps four million dollars over the next two days.

As the organizing auctioneer, Gunther would receive ten percent of the total commission, some three or four hundred thousand dollars. Few people knew that Gunther also owned forty percent of the business, having accumulated that from various members of Barnaby Barkley's family over the last twenty years. Even allowing for the expenses in researching the books, organizing the catalogues, generating the publicity, and running the auction, BB Bookshelf Auctions could earn three million dollars at this sale. Gunther's fees and ownership interest could generate over $1.5 million in the next two days.

Nobody messed with Gunther.

The sales sequence was alphabetical by author, which happened to result in the first few items being in the low end of the value range. This was perhaps a good thing as it let everyone settle in.

The first ten items, with prices between $1,500 and $8,000, generally sold within the range of the pre-auction estimates provided by the auction house, although in the upper part of that range. This seemed to settle down everyone as, perhaps, it meant there would be good value given and received, as opposed to some chaotic frenzy.

The most expensive item in that early going was the 1748 published journals of George Anson, the British naval captain who circumnavigated the world and hassled the Spanish, as had Francis Drake 150 years earlier, although he didn't discover many new areas, as James Cook would twenty-five years later. It sold for $8,000 due to its immaculate condition.

The first item that sold above its estimated range was the 1804 publication by John Barrow, *Travels in China*. In spite of some contested bidding by some avid New York collectors, Alan Page bought it for $7,500.

Arctic voyages by Beechey and Belcher in the 1800s; Belin sea charts from 1764; the late 1700s Pacific voyage and mutinous experiences of Bligh; the same-period French voyages around the world of Bougainville; they all sold at the top of their ranges, from $5,000 to $50,000.

There were a few smiles in the crowd when the 1624 book of logarithms by Henry Briggs sold for $20,000. Sure, it was historically significant in the annals of navigation, but it was just a book filled with numbers!

Louis Wing, who had purchased the Broughton journals from Margaret Thomas at the Los Angeles book fair in February for $30,000, was pleased to see a similar book sell for $38,000 here.

Then, the pace of the auction seemed to pick up. A few more valuable books appeared and the bidding intensified.

A classic volume by Samuel de Champlain, describing his voyages up the St. Lawrence River, and containing the first map to depict all of the Great Lakes, issued in 1632, had been expected to sell for about $250,000. Jeremy Boucher had arranged with one of his customers to bid up to $300,000. It sold for $425,000.

Shortly thereafter, a set of over 100 lithograph plates by Louis Choris was offered. Choris had sailed with the Russian explorer Kotzebue who circumnavigated the world from 1815 to 1818. His images were absolutely stunning, covering everywhere from South America, across the South Pacific, and to Siberia and Alaska. The pre-sale estimate was $150,000 to $200,000. Via Margaret Thomas, Louis Wing had to bid $325,000 to obtain the set.

A complete set of the three voyages of James Cook, including the atlas of maps and illustrations, all in great shape, of course, sold for $85,000. This was a bit of a surprise, since there were always Cook journals available in the market for $50,000 to $70,000.

Prices settled down a bit as volumes by Cortez, Coxe, Dampier, Darwin, and others were sold. Even the publication by Copernicus in 1540, which first defined a heliocentric model of the planetary system, i.e., the sun was at the center and Earth revolved around it, sold as predicted for $400,000 to Simon Katz

The last item before a break in the action was the four-volume set of nautical charts for the Atlantic coasts of North America published by Joseph Des Barres between 1774 and 1779 for the British Admiralty. They were detailed, accurate, and outstanding in their presentation. It was also the time of the outbreak of the American Revolution, and so they had historic and military significance.

Again, Jeremy Boucher had worked his network of Americana collectors. This time he was successful. Acting on behalf of a client in Baltimore, he had bid $900,000, the limit he had been given at two bids over the pre-sale upper estimate. He was thankful that no one had decided to make a statement by bidding a million dollars.

24

The auction had been going for two hours when Gunther Shultz called for a thirty-minute recess. One-quarter of the Cushing collection had been sold.

The break allowed everyone to stretch, use a washroom, and get a drink without missing any of the action.

As Gunther well knew, it also gave people time to chat and think. Almost everyone arrives at an auction with a focus on specific items and with a pre-set limit on what they will bid. Given time to absorb the bidding thus far, and to think about it for a short time, no one ever reduces their bid limit, but many people will talk themselves into higher levels. This break provided some time for that to happen.

Generally, as people mingled, they were relaxed and convivial. The results so far were at the upper end of forecast values, with a few outlier bids, but nothing outlandish. This was very positive for the auctioneers and for the Cushing family, since the upper estimates were intended to be a stretch.

Louis Wing and Margaret Thomas huddled in a corner.

"It's going well, don't you think?" offered Margaret.

"Yes," replied Louis. "The Choris was a bit pricey."

"It's truly an outstanding copy. Also, we have secured three other books on your list at reasonable prices."

"So far, so good."

Herb Trawets and Colin Mackenzie chatted briefly in the middle of the room.

"Prices are quite solid," ventured Colin. "They might not be the break-out I might have hoped for, but we will do well with our inventory."

Herb did not go anywhere near Louis Wing.

Jeremy Boucher took the time to phone the clients who had been behind some of his early bids to give them the results and to double-check with a few that supported upcoming ones.

His call to Baltimore had been upbeat, "We were successful! The Des Barres is yours."

"How much?"

"We had to go the limit; the competition is active here."

"OK," the client said, with a mixture of happiness and doubt. Buyer's remorse often sets in for a while after a large purchase.

Hadrian Wall, who had decided to come to New York for the sale at the last minute, talked with Chester Chalk. They hadn't bought anything yet; they hadn't even bid on anything seriously.

"What do you think, Cheese?" asked Hadrian.

"I think it's alright. There haven't been that many significant Arctic items yet, but, in general, prices are reasonable given the reputation and quality of the collection."

"Well, we'll see soon. Some of our items of interest will be coming up after the break."

Graham Maltsby was pleased. He had purchased the around-the-world volumes by Anson and Dampier for his inventory. He had also been the one who bid up the price for the James Cook voyages; he had a collector in Brisbane who was determined to get that particular set. Its provenance included being once owned by the buyer's great-grandfather, something that only mattered to him.

Stuart Scott was happy to have secured the Champlain volume for a client in Montreal.

Simon Katz quietly observed it all. He had purchased a few volumes but he was being careful. He had the sense that collectors were dominating so far, even if it was through brokering dealers. His only advantage was specific knowledge as opportunities arose.

The second session of the auction was announced.

Walking back into the auction hall, Simon Katz happened to encounter Herb Trawets.

With a smile and a wink, he said, "The next item should be fun, Herb."

Herb smiled back.

25

The next item to be offered was a complete set of the de Bry collections of English voyages published between 1590 and 1608. There were actually two subsets: *Great Voyages about the Americas* and *Small Voyages about the East Indies*. They were impressively bound in a total of 25 volumes. They were written in Latin.

This was expected to be the most expensive lot at the auction. The pre-sale estimate was $1.2-$1.4 million, although there had not been a complete set sold publicly for many decades to provide any reliable reference. The Streeter collection had not contained a de Bry set.

Simon Katz's aside comment to Herb Trawets referred to the private sale of a similar set that they had jointly brokered a couple of years ago, when then Vice-President Ray Cartwright purchased a set from the Armstrong family in Boston, the set that was now on loan to Harvard University.

Simon did not know what the final deal price had been between Cartwright and the Armstrongs. They had kept that secret, but he knew, based on the early positioning in the negotiations and the fees he and Herb were paid, that Ray Cartwright had paid at least $2 million.

Simon had cobbled together an arrangement with two other large dealers to bid on this. They had agreed to share equally up to $1.5 million. They also agreed that Simon could bid up to $2 million if he put up the difference himself, with their shares being adjusted accordingly.

Colin Mackenzie, who had no knowledge of the Cartwright-Armstrong deal, had similarly put together a partnership of London dealers. They were prepared to bid £1 million, equivalent to about $1.75 million.

Louis Wing wanted these books. He had decided that he would personally bid on three items, rather than bid through Margaret Thomas. He did want to enjoy the experience of bidding at such a high stakes event and, deep down, he did want to show off a little. The de Bry set was one of those three items.

Gunther Shultz was well aware that this item was going to attract a lot of attention. He had even tried to persuade his partners to indicate a higher expected price range, but they had opted to be more cautious. They believed that sellers were always happier to get more than expected rather than less than hoped for. Also, they believed it increased the reputation of any auction house to be able to proclaim they attracted higher prices than the market expected.

'Gunfire' Schultz even slowed down the pace for this item, which the audience noticed. It seemed to add to the drama. The de Bry bidding consumed almost two minutes.

The bidding started at one million dollars and went up in increments of $100,000.

A few different people made the first bids.

Then Simon entered at $1.4 million.

Colin: $1.5 million.

Simon: $1.6 million.

Colin: $1.7 million.

Simon: $1.8 million.

These bids had been paced out steadily, not rushed.

Then, after a somewhat longer pause, indicating to everyone that Colin had stopped, Louis raised his arm: $1.9 million.

Simon slowly looked over at Louis, who was looking back at him with a blank poker face. At that point Simon knew that Louis was not going to stop there. He could have raised the bid one more time to $2 million, but he knew it would be a waste of time. He also knew that Louis knew that Simon could have bid him up some more. Stopping now actually created a bit of goodwill with Louis, which could come in handy in the future.

With an almost imperceptible nod to Louis, Simon looked back at Gunther Shultz and shook his head.

Louis now owned the de Bry collection.

The de Bry sale also seemed to energize the rest of that day's action; prices hovered at or above the top of the estimates, thus being somewhat higher than the first session.

The Pacific voyage of Dixon sold briskly.

Simon Katz bought six publications on the mid-1700s controversy about the Arctic passage potential by Arthur Dobbs collectively for $200,000, a third higher than similar volumes had sold for at the Streeter sale.

The Arctic journal of Swaine Drage attracted many bids. Hadrian Wall, getting caught up in the auction, purchased it for $65,000, a bit more than he had originally intended to bid.

The next significant items were the Sir Francis Drake journals. There was the 1626 *Sir Francis Drake Revived*, which described his early Caribbean ventures against the Spanish, and the 1628 *World Encompassed*, which described his famous around-the-world voyage. Both of these had been published by his nephew three decades after his death.

The estimated prices for these items had ranged up to $25,000 for the first book and $250,000 for the second. They sold for 25 percent above that amount to Colin Mackenzie.

A short while later the 1735 du Halde about China sold for $60,000 to Alan Page. Simon noted that with interest; he had sold the same publication at the New York fair for $50,000. He deduced that the Chinese were buying these items and that Alan was acting for them. After all, Alan didn't buy items like that for himself, and he had also bought the Barrow item about China earlier. He tucked that information away for later use.

The Spanish publication by Espinosa, describing the late 1700s world expedition by Malaspina, sold for a respectable $100,000. Even the separate publication about the side trip by the explorers Galiano and Valdes, who were the first Europeans to circumnavigate Vancouver Island (in spite of the British legend of George Vancouver), sold for $40,000. Simon bought both.

The 1635 Arctic journal of Luke Foxe, one of the earliest Arctic adventurers, sold for $150,000 to Stuart Scott. Hadrian Wall had wanted that item but he balked after $140,000.

As the first day of the auction was nearing its conclusion, the Patrick Gass 1807 journal about the Lewis and Clark expedition was offered. This publication had not been authorized by Lewis and Clark, but it became famous and valued because it appeared years before their official publication.

George Archer, Jeremy Boucher, Margaret Thomas, Herb Trawets, Louis Wing, and many others watched the bidding closely. This item didn't have the special history and provenance of the upcoming actual Lewis and Clark journals, but it might offer some insight into that sale which would occur on day two of the auction.

Perhaps influenced by caution, the Gass sold for $50,000, right on the upper estimate. Jeremy Boucher purchased it for his client in St. Louis.

The last major item of the day was the 1589 Richard Hakluyt *Principal Navigations, Voyages and Discoveries of the English Nation*. It preceded the de Bry collection by a decade, and was perhaps the most famous book in the realm of travel and voyage book collecting. This volume included the Ortelius-based world map, the best such map of the time, and which is missing from almost every surviving copy of the book. It also contained the unnumbered, inserted six pages about Sir Francis

Drake's world voyage. The inclusion of those pages had been forbidden to Hakluyt by Francis Drake and, indirectly, by Queen Elizabeth.

As with the de Bry, Louis Wing bid on this book himself, and he again prevailed, bidding $375,000.

Day one of the auction ended. Sales had totalled just over $11 million. The pre-sale estimate up to this point had been $7.5 million to $10 million.

The Cushing family was happy.

26

As had happened during the mid-session break, but with more time to contemplate and plan for the next day's session, everyone took stock of the first day's results.

Louis Wing had been the dominant participant. With his open bidding on the de Bry and Hakluyt items and the bids that Margaret Thomas had made on his behalf, he had spent over one-quarter of the day's total, almost $3 million.

As he contemplated the second day, he was interested in a few expensive items, notably the Purchas and Warre items, but he was most anxious about the Lewis and Clark journals; they were as close to a one-of as anything else in the whole auction. He hoped that his planned ploy with Herb Trawets would carry the day.

Margaret Thomas was pleased. She had earned a significant fee in support of Louis Wing. He even paid her a commission on the ones he chose to bid himself, since she had consulted with him on everything at the sale.

She hoped that her subtle dishonesty about the Lewis and Clark journals wouldn't backfire. Louis was going to be the big success story at the sale; surely the loss of that one item wouldn't matter that much!

Hadrian Wall was unsettled about the day. He was used to interacting with dealers directly at book fairs, online, or through Chester. This was his first experience at an upscale auction. He was pleased to have bought the Drage, even if it was a bit more than he planned. He was also disappointed at missing out on the Foxe; that was a more difficult item to find. Tomorrow, he was determined to pursue the longitude Acts and the James journal.

Jeremy Boucher was satisfied. He had purchased the des Barres and Gass. He was a bit disappointed that the Champlain had eluded him, but he knew those things happened. He had instructions from clients for various items on tomorrow's agenda, notably the Harrison publications and the Lewis and Clark journals. Based on today's price trends, he felt he would be competitive.

Vancouver's Vengeance

Alan Page was comfortable. He had bought the few Chinese-related items at reasonable prices. There were some more significant items coming up.

Colin Mackenzie was happy with having purchased the Sir Francis Drake journals. He knew they would always have value. He had hoped to buy the de Bry collection, but knew that he would never have been able to compete with Louis Wing.

His decision to work with Yrrab Trawets to purchase an inventory of books before the sale looked solid. Prices had firmed up at the auction. They should be able to clear at least one third profit over the next year by remarketing the books, a nice profit of at least $1 million.

Stuart Scott was a bit surprised that he had bought the Champlain, the Foxe, and a few other minor books for just over a half-million dollars. He had expected the competition to be more aggressive.

Graham Maltsby had bought very little. Perhaps tomorrow.

Herb Trawets had nothing to plan; he only had one part to play in tomorrow's second act. He enjoyed a pleasant evening attending a Broadway play, *Lincoln*. He noted the slight irony of his being at that play the night before his acting role involving two other presidents, at least indirectly: Jefferson and Cartwright.

Simon Katz analyzed the day in detail. He was very disciplined in his approach.

He was happy to have bought the Copernicus; he believed it had a good upside value at other venues, perhaps being a bit out of place at this sale. His purchase of books such as the Dobbs and Espinosa seemed sound. Missing out on the de Bry books to Louis Wing was just the reality of the business.

He expected that tomorrow would be much the same.

He also contemplated how to capitalize on his new awareness of the Chinese interest in relevant books. He did have some similar books in inventory; perhaps he should talk to Alan Page. However, he would probably work his own network first and accumulate even more volumes.

Simon was always thinking of the longer-term implications.

27

Everyone gathered for the second day of the Cushing auction. The mingling and banter were perhaps a bit more relaxed than on the first day, probably because there had been no big surprises.

As Chester Chalk and Hadrian Wall were walking into the auction hall, Chester noticed Louis Wing entering a few steps ahead. He said to Hadrian something that many people were thinking.

"Hey, Stone. There's Louis Wing. He's certainly no chicken; I'll bet he spent $3 million yesterday."

"Right, Cheese. Let's hope we're chasing different items today. Otherwise, we'll be chicken soup."

Gunther Shultz called the session to order and the auction resumed.

Again, the day's activity began with a few minor items. Then the session focused on the publications of John Harrison from the 1700s, which related to his invention of the clock that forever improved the explorers' determination of longitude. These publications were rare and cherished by collectors.

There were five different documents from the 1760s. Each item generated active bidding, but, in every case, Simon Katz was the purchaser. He seemed determined to establish his presence early, perhaps to temper the later actions by others. He paid a total of $1.25 million.

The next item was the collection of British Parliament Acts related to the search for a solution to the longitude problem. They had been placed in the auction sequence here due to their connection with Harrison and the hope by the auction house that the Harrison values would rub off.

This was the set that Hadrian Wall wanted. He now wished that they had been placed somewhere else in the auction; the Harrison action had set some high expectations. Again, as with the Drage, and remembering the Foxe, he bid more than planned, but was actually quite excited and pleased when he won the bidding at $85,000.

After another sequence of good, but familiar books that attracted expected prices, the 1633 published journal of Thomas James was offered. As with the Foxe, this was one of the earliest Arctic adventures. It even had a catchy title, *The Strange and Dangerous Voyage of Captain Thomas James.*

Again Hadrian was anxious. This was the only remaining book in the auction that he really cared about.

Stuart Scott had purchased the Foxe on the first day and he wanted the James; they would make a nice complementary set for a collector.

Again, Stuart prevailed at $150,000. Chester had convinced Hadrian that they could find another James for a better price. That would turn out to be poor advice.

The next series of books included a number of Russian voyages in the Pacific during the 1800s: Kotzebue, von Kruzenstern, and Lisiansky. These sold at the top of the estimated range, totalling a bit over $100,000. Alan Page was the purchaser.

Simon Katz again observed that with interest. Alan was buying both Chinese and Russian publications.

Jean La Perouse was perhaps the most famous French explorer of the eighteenth century. He surveyed the Pacific in the 1780s, following on from Cook. He visited South America, California, Alaska, Siberia, Indonesia, and Australia. His ship was lost somewhere in the Far East but his journals survived, having been sent overland from Siberia to Paris in an epic multi-year trek. The maps and drawings that accompanied the journals are some of the best early renditions of those areas.

This auction item attracted bids from many people; the story had multi-national interest. Acting on behalf of a client in Sydney and buoyed by the Australian currency values, Graham Maltsby bought the set for $35,000.

Then it was time for the Lewis and Clark journals.

There seemed to be an added sense of anticipation in the room, driven by the feeling that this item was truly a part of American history, including the signatures of President Jefferson and William Clark. Most of the other items involved explorers from other places.

Louis Wing had positioned himself at the back of the room to be best able to watch the action. Herb Trawets was in the front row, slightly off to one side, where he could easily observe Margaret Thomas. Margaret was a few rows back on the other side; her associate, John Miller, was in the row in front of her.

Gunther Shultz, again sensing there would be some serious competition for this item, slowed down the pace as he had with the de Bry the day before.

Quite a few different hands were raised as the bid progressed from $250,000 in increments of $25,000.

Margaret Thomas, acting for Louis Wing: $350,000.

Jeremy Boucher, acting for his St. Louis client: $375,000.

Margaret: $400,000.

Jeremy: $425,000.

John Miller, acting for George Archer: $450,000.

There was a noticeable pause here. It became obvious that Margaret and Jeremy had reached their limit.

Herb Trawets, in the front row, slightly raised his hand, catching the attention of one of the auction-staff spotters: "475," said Gunther.

Most observers didn't know where the bid had come from. They had been focused on Margaret, Jeremy, and John. Their focus certainly stayed there now, waiting for the next response.

John Miller nodded: $500,000.

This time Herb raised his arm quite deliberately: $525,000.

There was a slight murmur from a number of people, certainly including the industry insiders such as Margaret, Jeremy, and Simon. They all had the same reaction: "President Ray Cartwright wanted this! It made sense; one President collecting an item from another President. Herb had always been the insider with Cartwright."

If any of them were tempted to bid more, they declined.

After the appropriate pause and quiet urging for another bid, Gunther simply said, "Sold. $525,000 to Mister Trawets."

At the back of the room, Louis Wing had a small smile on his face. The procedure that he and Herb had planned had worked perfectly.

The auction settled down for the next few items.

Hadrian Wall bought a signed copy of Mackenzie's 1801 publication of his overland journeys to the Arctic for $20,000.

Simon Katz bought the 1885 Malaspina journal for $10,000.

Alan Page, in an actively contested bidding session, bought the 1555 Marco Polo publication of his travels to China for $75,000.

Gunther then called the mid-session break.

The mingling and chatting during the break was similar to the day before. It included mild speculation about who had really bought the Lewis and Clark journals, but there was no confirmation to be had. Herb Trawets had quietly left.

One keen observer even asked the rhetorical question, "Why do most explorers have names starting with the first half of the alphabet? The auction is three-quarters done and we're only at M."

Another responded, "That may be true, but there are some big items still to come."

28

The final session of the Cushing auction opened with a bang.

The 1555 Martyr publication of voyages, notably the Pacific navigations and conquests of the Spanish, is a valuable and rare item. It preceded the Hakluyt and de Bry publications by decades. Published barely a half-century after the discovery voyage of Columbus, it was one of the very first English volumes to describe what degrees of longitude meant on a round world and to explain the workings of a compass for navigation.

Louis Wing wanted this item to complement his earlier purchases, and so bid the price to 25 percent over the high estimate; he paid $1 million.

A volume on navigation and a map of the Atlantic from the same vintage by Medina sold for $300,000 to Colin Mackenzie. He planned to package it as an item with the Drake books, since Francis Drake had taken a copy of that map with him on his famous voyage around the world; it was one of the few guides he had, even if it was relatively useless for actual navigation.

A late 1500s treatise on the history of China by Mendoza, the first substantial survey of China published in the west, was based on the travels of Augustine and Franciscan monks. It sold to Alan Page for $250,000.

Various volumes on the exploration of the Pacific by Meares, Muller, and Portlock and of the Arctic by McClure, Middleton, Parry, and Peary all sold for high-range prices.

The last notable early collection of voyages was the 1626 Samuel Purchas *Pilgrimes*, published forty years after Hakluyt and containing more voyages, many impressive maps, and interpretive comments by Purchas. Again, Louis set out to complete his set, paying $400,000 this time.

Many landmark Arctic volumes sold well: Rae, Ross, Richardson, Scoresby, and Seeman. Alan Page again bought some Russian Pacific explorations by Sarychev and Shelekhov.

At one point there was an active bidding contest between Hadrian Wall and Colin Mackenzie over a relatively minor item, a couple of weekly journals published by Charles Dickens in the mid-1850s.

The most significant event in the history of Arctic exploration was the 1845 voyage by Sir John Franklin in search of the missing link for a Northwest Passage across the top of America. After leaving England and briefly stopping on the coast of Greenland, the expedition was never seen again.

By 1847, when no word had been heard from Franklin, the British Admiralty and his family decided that a rescue mission should be sent out. In fact, over the next twelve years more than fifty expeditions headed to the Arctic in search of Franklin. Those voyages essentially defined the Arctic, and the journals of those expeditions are what constitute the heart of any Arctic rare book collection.

In 1854, John Rae, one of the most accomplished Arctic explorers, was travelling across the Boothia Peninsula when he heard tales from some natives about a large group of Europeans who had starved to death years earlier, many days' journey farther west of that location. The natives also had artifacts that they said came from the site. Being very late in the summer season, the Eskimos were unwilling to travel back to that area. Rae returned to England with the story of the probable fate of Franklin.

Rae had brought back other details of Franklin's fate, based on the stories of the natives. Apparently, Franklin's crew had resorted to cannibalism in their final days. Rae included all of this in his report to the British Admiralty. The content of the report became public.

The reaction was immense. It was an extreme example of "shooting the messenger." No one wanted to believe that British naval officers and men would do such a thing. Rae was accused of many things, among them: being a liar; being a crook trying to claim the reward for determining Franklin's fate; being a coward for coming back to England without travelling farther to confirm the information; and being a dupe for believing the tales of the unreliable natives.

One of the most outspoken critics of John Rae's report was Charles Dickens. At the time he was the publisher of a weekly journal called *Household Words*. In a series of articles over three issues of that journal in late 1854, Dickens soundly criticized Rae for his conclusions about cannibalism, stoutly defending the honor of the navy and castigating the savage natives as being thieves, liars, and worse. Rae wrote some rebuttals. After a pause, and in response to a submission by Rae, Dickens actually published Rae's full report to the Admiralty in February, 1855. After all, Dickens was in the business of selling his weekly journals.

In this environment, Rae's journals of his extensive travels were never formally published and he, almost alone among the many captains of Arctic expeditions, was never awarded any honors.

Years later, in 1859, Leopold McClintock would confirm Franklin's fate, and therefore Rae's report, by discovering the site of the crew's final encampment.

Vancouver's Vengeance

The Cushing collection contained a copy of all the relevant issues of the Dickens journals. They were essentially small, thin, paper-covered pamphlets. In the last volume was Dickens' signature below a dedication to Rae, which made it unique.

Hadrian wanted the collection as a key Arctic item. Colin wanted it for a client in London who collected anything Dickensian. An unsigned set of these volumes would normally sell for up to $2,000. The auction house had estimated that the signature would increase its value to $5,000. Hadrian Wall paid $12,000.

The George Vancouver journals have always sold at the upper end of value compared to the many other Pacific explorers of the late 1700s, even over a full set of the three voyages of James Cook. This reflects the limited number of copies available. There was only one edition of the full-sized, quarto journals, accompanied by a folio-sized atlas of the quality maps and illustrations, issued. That was in 1798, shortly after Vancouver's death. A second, smaller-sized octavo issue followed in 1801.

The specific volumes in the Cushing collection had one extra dimension that increased their value: their special binding.

Antiquarian books are often rebound over time. Good rebinding is done in the style of the original date of publication and with high quality materials.

In the eighteenth century, no leather was finer than that made in Russia. Using reindeer hides and special treatments, the leather had a beautiful red hue and pleasant aroma. It was supple and water-resistant.

In 1786 a Baltic brigantine carrying such Russian leather to Italy sank off the coast of England in a violent storm. Almost two hundred years later, the ship, *The Metta Catherina*, was found by divers. To the amazement of everyone, many bundles of the quality leather were found intact, preserved by the sea water and seafloor sediments. It was highly valued for its quality and history, and was used by leatherworkers to make upscale shoes, purses, briefcases, and belts.

Reginald Cushing had purchased some of that salvaged leather and he had the Vancouver volumes rebound with it. After all, the leather's age was almost identical to that of the books.

Chester Chalk, after determining that Hadrian Wall was not interested in the volumes since he already had a set and was not that interested in the special leather, had arranged to act for another collector from Vancouver. After some lively bidding, he was successful at a price of $120,000.

A copy of the Viana journal, related to the 1789 Malaspina expedition, and being one of the rarest volumes related to the early exploration of

Australia and the northwest of America, sold to Graham Maltsby for $45,000.

The final high-value item offered in the auction was the 1848 collection of beautiful colored sketches of the Canadian prairies, the Rocky Mountains, and the Oregon territories by Henry Warre. Everyone who sees these images always describes them as magnificent.

Simon Katz, Jeremy Boucher, and Colin Mackenzie were all interested, but Stuart Scott, acting on behalf of a determined collector from Calgary who considered the images to be local art, won out at $250,000.

The auction was over. Sales exceeded the predicted upper range of $20 million by $3 million. It may not have been as surprising as the Streeter results in 2007, but, nevertheless, it was impressive.

Most everyone was satisfied. Of course, as always, people wondered if they had paid too much for something they had bought, or questioned whether or not they should have bid more for something they hadn't.

As Gunther Shultz closed the session, he made an announcement.

"There will be a one-day auction of an outstanding collection of books and ephemera linked to the general exploration of the Pacific coast of America and, in particular, related to the explorer George Vancouver. The sale will take place in Vancouver, Canada, early next year. A catalogue of that collection is now available at our website; hard copies will be available within a week. I'll see you there."

BOOK TWO

The Second Auction

29

The catalogue for the auction of antiquarian books and ephemera related to George Vancouver was a surprise to everyone. In the aftermath of the Cushing auction there was a general expectation that it would pale by comparison; it didn't.

The collection was smaller than the Cushing one, with only two hundred items, due to the more limited scope of the collection. It centered on the exploration of the north Pacific from the fifteenth to nineteenth centuries. It didn't have many items related to the Arctic or general world exploration.

The collection had been assembled by a recently-deceased forest industry executive, George Douglas, a Vancouver, British Columbia, native who had developed a keen interest in local history. He had assembled it over many years, initially during trips to Europe, and in later decades at book fairs, online searches, auctions, and with the help of a few book scouts. Somehow he had managed to keep a low profile within the book-collecting world and, thus, even the main dealers hadn't realized the extent and quality of his collection. In particular, he had focused on volumes that had been signed by the author, a factor that always increased a book's value.

The exploration of the North Pacific attracted the attention of collectors with many different interests, including world exploration, North American history, the Pacific-Rim nations of China and Russia, and the search for an Arctic northwest passage between the Atlantic and Pacific oceans.

More than half of the books were the same publications as ones that had been in the Cushing sale. The auctioneer's pre-sale price estimates were directly based on the Cushing results. This was an amazing feat of logistics for BB Bookshelf Auctions. They had monitored the Cushing sale results and had modified the Vancouver sale estimates in real time. This explained why the catalogue was only available online immediately, with hard copies to take a week longer.

A book that sold for $10,000 at the Cushing sale was estimated as $8,000 to $12,000. This reinforced the image of quality, gave the selling family a reasonable expectation, and stimulated buyers to think upside.

At first glance, it was not obvious why BB Bookshelf Auctions had chosen to emphasize the sale as a Vancouver sale, rather than as a Pacific Northwest Exploration sale, or even the Douglas sale.

It was because there was one item that astounded everyone—a signed copy of George Vancouver's journals!

This totally contradicted history. George Vancouver had died before his journals were published.

The sale catalogue dedicated ten pages to the set.

It began with the traditional short description of Vancouver's voyage and then described the journals. There were three volumes that described Vancouver's journey and all of the places he visited and sights he saw in great detail. The key element was the large folio-sized fourth volume that held the attractive maps and illustrations of geographic scenes across the Pacific and along the American coast.

The catalogue's text then provided a summary of the reasons for the historically high values placed on Vancouver sets—their information and beauty, combined with the fact there had only been one limited-edition run printed in 1798. Demand for them in the early 1800s had not been great, and the plates had somehow been lost, or destroyed, before anyone wanted to print more. A second, smaller-format version had been printed in 1801, but it did not have the same interest or collector value as these original sets.

Interestingly, the auction house did not provide a price estimate. It simply noted that similar, unsigned sets had sold in recent times for $75,000 to $120,000, with the latter price being for the Russian-leather-bound set at the Cushing sale.

The history of the specific books was not clear. An invoice from a London book dealer dated 1946 included an item, *Vancouver files*, along with a number of other exploration volumes. It showed a price of £400.

The catalogue included many pages of information, analyses, high-resolution photographs, and testimonials from experts that served to verify the authenticity of the documents and the signatures.

In fact, the documents were not bound books. They were a loose pile of printed page-sets, untrimmed, and contained in small, properly-sized cardboard sleeves. These were the proof-sets that the printer had provided to George and John Vancouver for approval before printing the final sets.

George Vancouver's signature of approval was on the covering pages of the first two volumes. His brother John, who had assisted him with the editing, had endorsed the third volume and the folio set.

The accompanying materials asserted that the paper, type-set, and ink were identical to that used in the actual journals that were published.

The ink used for Vancouver's signature was identical to the ink on verified letters that he had written in 1797 and 1798.

Handwriting experts attested to the authenticity of the signatures.

The signed journals were real.

30

The Vancouver journals created quite a stir in the book-collecting world. Of course, everyone, dealers and collectors alike, started to speculate on what the auction price would be and whether or not they could participate.

The question is often asked, "How many copies of a certain old publication actually exist?" Usually no one knows. Even if there is a record of how many were created in the first place, which is not usually the case for very old books, it is impossible to know how many still exist, let alone in what degrees of completeness or condition. Sometimes most known copies are sequestered in national museums or major university collections where they are not likely to become available to private collectors. The antiquarian book world determines rarity by how often a certain book appears in the marketplace, such as in dealers' catalogues, at book fairs, in auctions, or on websites such as Book Finder and Abe Books. Of course, unknown numbers sit dormant in the libraries of old family estates or the forgotten basement stacks in old bookstores. That's how surprises happen.

There are very few examples in the book world where there is truly a one-of-a-kind. After all, books, by definition, are designed to be mass produced. Singular items arise either because other copies have been lost over the years or because they have some special provenance. The Vancouver journals with the signatures filled both criteria. Being the printer's proof set they had a singular status, and with the signatures they had unequalled provenance.

The price for such an item is established by the most determined buyer with the most collection-available money. This sets the high prices you often read about, such as $50 million for a van Gogh painting or $3 million for a Honus Wagner baseball card.

In the book-collecting world, a perfect example is the 2013 auction of a copy of the *Bay Psalm Book*. It is a very small volume printed in 1640 by the Congressional Puritans in Cambridge, Massachusetts. Originally, 1740 copies were printed, but only eleven have survived, and most of those copies are now closely held in university libraries and the Library of Congress. The books were used routinely in the church for many years and so the surviving copies show excessive signs of wear. Nevertheless, the book sold for over $20 million.

Vancouver's Vengeance

The demand for the book had nothing to do with its content or condition. It appealed to every book collector; it was the first book ever printed in the United States.

Simon Katz, in New York, considered the situation. He had no idea what the winning bid for the Vancouver journals would be, but he knew it would be set by a wealthy collector, not a dealer. The journals would attract absolute full value; there would be no margin left for a speculative, reselling-based purchase.

Simon had connections with many wealthy collectors. He needed to scan his network for an opportunity to provide advice and bidding support. He realized, with some regret, that the two most likely big bidders were Louis Wing and Ray Cartwright, and they both had closer links to other dealers.

Colin Mackenzie, in London, reached the same conclusion. Nevertheless, he started to contact his key customers.

Hadrian Wall, in Vancouver, talked over the situation with Chester Chalk. He was totally intrigued by the journals. He knew that he would love to own them, but he also knew that he was not likely to be willing to spend enough to buy them. After all, he hadn't even been tempted to upgrade his set of Vancouver journals to the Russian leather ones in the Cushing auction. But, these were different.

"Cheese, what do you think it will take to buy them?"

"I don't know. Usually books with special provenance will attract a premium of 25 to 50 percent, but we have seen much larger premiums, such as the Lewis and Clark journals at the Cushing sale. I bought the Vancouver set at Cushing for $120,000; I expect this set could go for twice that, or more."

"I know that's true. If I thought $125,000, or even $150,000, would be enough, I'd be very tempted. But that would be it, even in the excitement of an auction."

"Do you want to wait and see, to try that?" asked Chester. His first allegiance in all his dealer-customer relationships was to Hadrian Wall.

"No. I know it won't be enough. You had another customer who bought the Cushing set. You should feel free to work with him, or anyone else you think might be interested."

"Thanks, Stone. I appreciate that, but I doubt if I will get the necessary interest in this set. It'll be pricey."

Vancouver's Vengeance

Louis Wing's conversation with Margaret Thomas had a somewhat different tone, although it started out in the same way.

"Louis, I don't have any idea what the winning bid will be. You and a few other keen collectors will inevitably end up setting the limit. You all know how unique the set is and how badly you want to have them.

"I cannot give you any kind of informed estimate. Perhaps we could analyze the potential competition, but even that's not particularly useful. There are many determined collectors in the world. This set will certainly appeal to many traditional British collectors and there are new collectors appearing in the Middle East and China; we are flying blind."

"Right. I'll just have to check my bank account," Louis said with a smile.

Jeremy Boucher concluded that he was unlikely to get a competitive mandate from any of his major contacts, since most of them were totally focused on the exploration and history of the United States, not Canada. However, he would contact them, just in case one was interested.

Again, Mr. Wu contacted Alan Page and they went through the auction catalogue. They identified a few books to pursue, but, to Alan's disappointment, Mr. Wu was not interested in the Vancouver journals.

"George Vancouver's voyage didn't include a stop in China," was his simple explanation.

Alan had dreamt of earning a big commission on the purchase of such a valuable item, remembering that Mr. Wu simply bid whatever it took to win.

31

Although he was retired and no longer an active player, Herb Trawets studied the list of books with interest and with a bit of nostalgia. His involvement with the Cushing sale had been stimulating.

He was as surprised and as intrigued by the Vancouver journals as anyone. This was an item that broke from all of the conventional wisdom for over two hundred years.

He wondered if President Cartwright would be interested in the set, although his lack of pursuit of the Lewis and Clark books at the Cushing sale probably indicated he would not be. Nevertheless, he would contact the President's office again; to not do so would be out of the norm. He had consistently kept Cartwright apprised of significant items that appeared in the market.

A week later, coordinated again by Elsie Browning, Herb received a scheduled phone call from Ray Cartwright.

After some quick pleasantries, Ray asked, "Tell me about the books you mentioned to Elsie."

Herb described the Vancouver journals and the surprising presence of the signatures.

"That is fascinating. You know, I could be interested. They are obviously truly one-of-a-kind. Even the Lewis and Clark books at the Cushing sale were one of a small number of other similar copies."

After a pause, he continued with the obvious question, "What do you think they will sell for?"

Herb replied as everyone else, asked the same question, had. "I don't know. Well over the $120,000 paid for the Cushing set, but it will depend on the competition for such a unique item."

"Right! I'll need to think about my limit for a while. Can you send me a copy of the auction catalogue so that I can read up on the details of the set?"

"Sure thing. I'll courier a copy today. It's also available for browsing online at BB Bookshelf Auctions."

"Thanks. I'll be in touch again, probably next week."

After they concluded the phone call Herb sat still for a few minutes, unsuccessfully trying to determine why he had a sudden feeling of unease. Perhaps he was just surprised by Ray Cartwright's renewed interest.

32

Louis Wing couldn't stop thinking about the Vancouver journals. He really wanted to buy them and he knew he would pay top dollar. However, what could he do to mitigate an uncontrolled bidding war?

He was well aware of the stories that circulate in the antique dealers' world about groups of dealers collaborating to buy an item at an auction without competing with each other and then, later, re-auctioning or joint-selling it among themselves. This kept more of the profits within their group. This concept was likely more legend than reality, at least in modern times, with all of the open communications and internet listings that make essentially every major auction accessible to a multitude of dealers and collectors worldwide. There is always active competition. That doesn't preclude joint bidding to preserve capital or share risk, of course.

He had always enjoyed watching the British television series, *Lovejoy*, which depicted the shadier side of the antique dealer world of England. Lovejoy was a wheeler-dealer, scheming scoundrel that viewers came to like, something like J. R. Ewing or Maverick in America. Lovejoy was often shown manipulating antique sales.

Louis knew that there would be keen interest in the journals and, as Margaret Thomas had said, a lot of unknowns in Britain and Asia. However, for some reason, he felt the real competition would be North American. Vancouver wasn't that famous or popular a person generally, but his name was better known in association with the Canadian city and landmarks.

At the Cushing sale he had shown that he was willing to be more aggressive than others in his bidding; he had bought many of the expensive items. That should mean he had an advantage again. After all, he had plenty of discretionary money.

In thinking it through more carefully, he recognized that his biggest competitor could be Ray Cartwright. He also had the money and the general interest.

However, he had not participated at the Cushing sale, as borne out by the fact that Herb Trawets was available to act as his secret agent for the Lewis and Clark purchase. Margaret Thomas was still not aware of what had actually happened there. She probably assumed, as did many others, that Cartwright had been the real purchaser. He didn't know whether

Herb's surprising involvement at the late stages of the bidding really saved him anything, but he knew it didn't cost him anything.

"Could I pull off something similar with the Vancouver set?" he mused.

He decided that his first action would be to contact Herb Trawets and to inquire if he was available to work with him at the Vancouver auction, as he had last time. This would immediately tell him if Ray Cartwright was planning to participate at the next sale.

He made the phone call.

"Hi, Herb. It's Louis Wing here."

"Hello, Louis. How are you?"

"Just fine. I wanted to call and thank you again for your help at the Cushing sale. That worked out great."

"You're welcome. I agree," responded Herb, cautiously. What was Louis up to?

"I'm sure you have seen all the information about the auction in Canada. I was wondering if you would be available to work with me again."

Herb paused, thinking, "Ouch. There it is! He might as well have asked me directly if Ray Cartwright was going to bid."

Then, carefully controlling his tone, he replied candidly, "Louis, I don't know, and I can't answer that question. I need to keep myself free of conflicts at this point."

Herb hoped he had not given anything away.

Louis, with his antennae fully tuned, thought, "OK. Cartwright's a player."

"I understand, Herb. Let's keep in touch. Thanks."

After mulling over many possibilities, a couple of days later Louis called Herb again.

After the usual greetings, he said, pausing along the way, "Herb, hear me out about a hypothetical situation.

"We know that there will be a great deal of interest in the Vancouver journals from around the world.

"We also know that, in these circumstances, bidding will eventually come down to the two people who have the most interest and the most money. They can get carried away at times in the heat of an auction. That's why a Picasso painting sold for millions of dollars in London last month.

"Sometimes, two interested parties get together to joint-bid on an item, giving them more fire power to bid against the opposition, and giving them a chance to at least share the item.

"Would you know of any situation where something like that could happen here?"

Herb was flabbergasted.

How should he react? What could he possibly say? Should he just end the conversation immediately?

"Louis, I understand it's a hypothetical question," he started, buying some more time to think.

"How could such a thing work? How would you set a price? How do you share a set of books?" he continued, bolder than he expected.

Louis smiled to himself. At least he hadn't been rebuffed right off.

"I guess there are many ways. For example, the parties could agree on a maximum price to bid and then have one of them do the actual bidding. If they're successful, they could time-share the books or could have a second auction between themselves to determine the owner.

"Or, they could conduct a simple put-option exercise. Each one privately writes down their maximum bid. The person with the higher value buys out the other one at the lower value. It keeps both people very honest."

Trying to think all of this through quickly, Herb replied, "I would think, in this circumstance, that it would be difficult to set an absolute maximum bid for the public auction. The action could stimulate one of the parties to want to up the limit."

Here, Louis made his big pitch. "Herb, I don't think I will have a limit. But to help control a possible uncontrolled situation, I would agree to joint-bid, up to a limit set by another large player. If the action forces the bid level even higher, I would be on my own."

Herb swallowed hard. Louis had just told him that he was going to bid a huge amount, whatever that meant.

"Louis, let me think about it."

Herb knew that he was essentially telling Louis that he would likely pass on the information and the offer to Ray Cartwright.

"Fine. Call me back when you can."

Herb didn't know what to do.

What was Louis up to? He certainly said he was going to bid big. Why suggest a joint venture? Did he just want to cut the process down to two bidders who could keep some of the value between them? Was he just fishing for competitive information? Was he thinking about using Herb again as a distraction?

Certainly, joint bidding was quite common for expensive items. It wasn't illegal. It wasn't even unethical when it was done to pool resources in order to make a competitive bid. The ethical line was less clear when both parties had adequate funds and it might be looked on as a restraint of competition. However, even then it could be seen as an opportunity to joint-own and joint-enjoy an item that only one of them could do otherwise. A bidding war only has one winner, the seller. The winning buyer can also be the real loser if the bid is too high.

In any case, after he thought it through, he knew that he couldn't ignore the proposition. He had to inform Ray Cartwright and see what he wanted to do.

Again, he arranged a phone call.

"Hi, Herb. Thanks for sending the catalogue. The Vancouver journals are certainly intriguing. They will go for a big price," opened the President.

"Right. That's why I had to talk to you and share something that's come up."

Herb then went on to describe his conversation with Louis Wing.

Ray Cartwright quietly contemplated what he had just heard. He didn't even bother to ask any questions; he knew exactly what was being proposed.

Finally, he said, "Herb, the answer is clear to me. I would like to own the set of books, but I would only be willing to pay so much, perhaps $200,000, or maybe $250,000. Louis has essentially told us he will pay more. I think I should just pass on the whole auction. I don't think of this as Louis having scared us off; I just think it's realistic. I suspect there will even be others who will bid more than I suggested."

Herb accepted the answer with a private smile. He realized that President Cartwright had just made a good decision, without even having to acknowledge there might have been an unethical proposal before him. He was a smart leader and politician.

Herb then called Louis back and, in a direct tone, told him, "I can't think of anyone who might want to joint venture with you on the Vancouver journals."

He then added, "Oh, by the way, I would be available to work with you, if you want."

Louis replied, "I'll be in touch." He hung up very satisfied.

33

President Cartwright was at home in Seattle with his wife, Anne, on a pre-Christmas break. They would spend Christmas at the White House with their children and grandchildren; that was a treat for them all. He always welcomed a chance to get away from Washington, however, even though the messages, briefing books, and security agents were still constantly present.

Looking in the mirror that morning, he noted a little more gray in his sideburns. He had always been amused by the photos of past Presidents that showed them aging over their years in office; here he was doing the same thing. However, he was approaching sixty. Compared to some of the previous Presidents, who had security crises or economic meltdowns to contend with, his tenure had been relatively calm. However, as always, the job was intense and nonstop. There were so many dimensions: domestic, international, and political, all involving many people, meetings, and decisions. But, of course, he looked forward to running for re-election soon.

Sitting in his office, his mind wandered to his antiquarian book collection, which he kept there. He enjoyed browsing through the old volumes, reliving the adventures and discoveries of past explorers.

He reflected back on the Cushing auction and the forthcoming Vancouver sale, which he had recently talked to Herb about. He was experiencing some "collector's regret" for not participating. There were some books that he would have liked to purchase. He had been distracted and probably too cautious about getting involved. After all, every voter knew that he was a wealthy man.

He once again retrieved his secret Sir Francis Drake document from the locked cabinet and reread the unknown story that it revealed about the extent of Drake's travels to the Pacific coast of North America.

He realized that, if this story was known, much of the context and hype about the voyages by Cook and Vancouver would change. With that thought in mind, he looked back at the auction catalogue for the Vancouver sale and, in particular, at the description of the George Vancouver journals.

He mused that the stories of the Vancouver and Drake documents had many parallels. Neither had been known to exist for centuries—over three hundred years for Drake and two hundred years for Vancouver. Now the world at least knew about the Vancouver journals.

As he read through the accompanying reports that testified to the authenticity of the Vancouver journals, he suddenly had a sinking feeling in his stomach. He wasn't sure why. Then he realized that, by comparison, the Drake document had not been subjected to the same level of investigation. In the name of secrecy, he had not been thorough.

When the document had been offered to him by Alan Page, acting for an unidentified seller, secrecy had been an unconditional requirement.

He had laboratory analyses of the paper, ink, and leather binding that showed they were old, and he had the type form verified as being of a style used three hundred years ago, but that was nothing close to the scrutiny the Vancouver documents had been through. The Vancouver specific paper, ink, and type were exactly matched to known authentic documents. The journals had been examined by experts and the signatures were meticulously examined. Ray had not shown the Drake document to anyone, and now he realized that it wasn't even signed; it had a typeset name at the end.

Surely he was just being paranoid.

Ray Cartwright continued to stare at the Sir Francis Drake document that, just minutes ago, he was admiring so much. Now, he was uncertain.

What if it was a fake? Had he been duped out of three million dollars? What should he do? Should he tell someone? Who? Were there political ramifications for re-election? How would voters judge the competence of a President who could be deceived like that?

All of those thoughts raced through his mind.

Taking a deep breath, he said to himself, almost out loud, "Whoa! Slow down. You are jumping to conclusions based on some unproven gut feelings. Check the facts and make a plan, just as you would for any other situation."

He took out some paper and started to make some lists. First of all, who knew about the Drake document?

As he thought back over the events that led to his acquisition of the document, he realized that, in fact, only Alan Page had briefly seen the document with him. Even then, Alan presumably did not know exactly what the document was.

Herb Trawets had been very involved with his raising the money to pay for the transaction, but he didn't know anything about the actual document, just that it was somehow related to Sir Francis Drake.

Simon Katz and the Armstrong family had been involved with his deferred purchase of the de Bry volumes, but they had no inkling about the Drake document or any of the financial manipulations that Ray and Herb had subsequently orchestrated behind the scenes to buy it.

His personal assistant, Maria Rodriguez, had similarly been purposely kept out of the loop.

Jeremy Boucher had been asked about methods to verify old documents but there had been nothing specific shared.

The laboratory tests had been done in commercial establishments using samples he sent. They had not seen the source material.

Ray had done a good job keeping the document secret, which, of course, was the objective at the time.

Who could he trust now?

Herb Trawets was his first thought.

Herb was certainly an expert in the area, had been his mentor as he created his collection over the years, and was proven to be trustworthy, as demonstrated with the money-raising escapade.

However, he wasn't comfortable getting Herb involved yet. Perhaps it was to avoid the embarrassment of having Herb, a close confidant in a way, discover that Ray had been duped. Perhaps it was that Herb was the only one, other than Alan Page, who knew how much money was involved. Ray could keep that part confidential, at least for now.

He instead decided that he would approach Jeremy Boucher. Jeremy was certainly an expert, with a reputation for fastidiousness and honesty. Ray had to know whether or not the Drake document was genuine.

Setting up a meeting would not be too difficult. After all, what President of the United States, planning to run for re-election, didn't visit Ohio a lot?

34

In early January, they met in Ray's hotel suite in Columbus. He was there to address a manufacturers' convention.

Ray had brought the Drake document and all of the previous analyses with him; he wanted to be sure to get the correct answer this time.

"Jeremy, thank you for coming to meet with me."

"You are very welcome, Mr. President. It's my honor," replied Jeremy, not quite sure why he was there.

"I have a situation that you can help me with, on a very discreet basis, if you are willing."

"If I can help you, sir, I would be pleased to do so."

"Well, simply put, I have a document in my possession and I am not sure it's genuine. I would like you to evaluate it and give me your professional opinion."

"I would be happy to do that."

"To be clear, you can take all the time you need and can arrange for any scientific or other tests that you deem appropriate. I will just ask you to keep the actual nature of the document and its content to yourself. Don't seek out other opinions, at least for now."

"OK," he replied, a little confused.

"Jeremy, the document I have is represented as having been created by Sir Francis Drake shortly before his death, elaborating on the journey to the Pacific that he took in the late 1570s. No record of the document exists."

Jeremy was momentarily speechless. Of course, he had never heard of such a document; he had never even heard of a rumor about it.

"So, you want me to examine it and to give you my opinion before you buy it? I can do that, but I suspect, if it is at all likely to be authentic, that you will want to get other opinions. The obvious question is how can it have existed for centuries in secret?"

"I wish it was quite that simple. No, I actually bought it a couple of years ago. Now I'm having second thoughts."

Jeremy suddenly had a memory of the few general inquiries from Ray Cartwright back then.

Ray continued, "The document was offered on the condition that it was to be kept completely secret. The implication was that the seller wanted to avoid publicity about its existence, and certainly its disposal, for family reasons. I bought the story. I had a number of tests done, which are described in the package of materials that I also have to give you."

"I expect I will have many questions when I get going. Getting more information on its provenance, or at least family history, would be one area of obvious investigation."

"I am afraid there's no more information about that. I don't even know who I bought the document from," Ray admitted, quite sheepishly. "You will need to rely on your own research, analyses, and experience. Then, it will come down to your opinion."

"I can give it a try, Mr. President.

"That's all I can ask. Of course, I will pay all of your direct costs and a professional service fee; would $50,000 cover the latter? You are the expert."

"That would be more than fair," replied Jeremy. It felt strange to be getting money from a politician, not donating to one.

"Good. Once you have completed your work, contact my office. We will organize another meeting. Thanks, Jeremy."

35

Jeremy Boucher was a bit overwhelmed with the task he had been given. How do you give a definitive answer to the President of the United States on something that's always subject to a fair amount of uncertainty?

The first thing he did, quite naturally, was to read the document. He immediately understood the significance of its content; after all, he was an expert in the history of exploration and discovery, and few explorers were more famous than Sir Francis Drake.

He had enough knowledge about the controversy about Drake's actual voyage path to know that the content was feasible. He also knew that the content had almost nothing to do with its authenticity, unless it could be shown to be absolutely false. After all, any decent forger should be able to get that part right.

In reading the document, he also got his first impression of its makeup and layout—the paper, typeset, binding, and general style. Although he was determined to keep an open mind until he could conduct a thorough analysis, his instincts told him there were some problems.

He read the technical reports that Ray Cartwright had provided him. He recognized that although they did not contain anything that would disprove the authenticity of the document, they also were very general and did not prove anything positive. This was not surprising, since Ray had only provided a few selective material samples to them for analysis. He had obviously very strictly kept the confidentiality requirement.

Then he laid out an analysis protocol. He had no concerns about how extensive or expensive that was. It wasn't just that he knew the President was wealthy, nor that he had already agreed to pay Jeremy a very generous fee; he knew from the nature of the document that the President had undoubtedly paid a lot for it, possibly millions.

The work would involve scientific analyses at leading laboratories and some time-consuming grunt work researching specific printing styles, fonts, and layouts from the 1500s. For the latter, he could use his connections with the history and literature departments at Ohio State University. There were always available graduate students who would take on projects for decent pay, and who would not need to be briefed on the real reasons for the work. Jeremy estimated that the project would take at least a month. He wasn't going to do anything but a thorough job.

He passed on a message about the timing to Ray Cartwright, who was not surprised that it would take that long. If anything, Ray treated the news as positive. At least Jeremy hadn't declared it a fake on first inspection!

36

Ray Cartwright and Jeremy Boucher met again in late January in Washington. Jeremy flew from Columbus.

Jeremy entered Ray's personal White House office carrying a large briefcase. It contained the Drake document, Ray's original reports, and two binders of new reports.

Of course, the briefcase had been inspected by the President's security detail, but they only checked for physical threats. They didn't focus on the content of papers or threats to the President's financial status or credibility. The people who worried about that sort of thing were not here. They didn't even know about the meeting.

Ray knew the answer the minute that Jeremy walked into the room. When people meet with the President of the United States, whether formally, politically, or socially, their body language always conveys their feelings. Although Jeremy looked composed, Ray could detect that he was nervous, perhaps even a bit afraid. That could mean only one thing.

"Jeremy, welcome again and thank you for coming. I know you have been very busy since we last met."

"Hello, Mr. President. It's good to see you."

"Well, Jeremy, let's get to it. What have you found?" Ray had used the word "found" rather than "decided," hoping to put Jeremy at ease a bit.

"Sir, would you like me to take you through our analyses before we try to reach any conclusions?" asked Jeremy.

"You know, that is almost always the way I work issues. It ensures we get the facts out before we start to debate opinions and try to reach consensus on a decision. However, I don't think that's necessary here. Please give me your conclusion and then we can fill in the details." This time, using "conclusion" rather than "opinion" again was designed to help Jeremy relax.

In fact, it did. Right then, Jeremy knew that Ray Cartwright knew the answer. He wasn't going to shoot the messenger.

"Mr. President, there is almost no possibility that the Drake document is genuine."

There it was!

Ray had known the answer he was going to get. Yet, it still felt like a blow to the stomach. What a fool!

Very quietly, Ray said, "Jeremy, thank you for being direct. Now, I truly would like to hear about your findings."

Over the next hour, Jeremy led Ray through all of the research and analyses.

First of all, he explained how the content of the document was not a consideration since it might all be true.

"Legitimate content does not make a document legitimate. Recall books such as the faked diaries of Adolf Hitler and Howard Hughes. To the reading public, they were credible.

"I found nothing that could be proven to be false, given all of the historic controversies. I read the text in detail, and cross-checked it with many references. I might even conclude that there is a slight bias in favor of the document, since it describes a second stop on the coast of California in the last stages of the voyage that would explain some of the contradictions in other accounts."

Then he addressed the paper.

"As your earlier analyses determined, the paper is definitely from Drake's time. It's the makeup that's the problem. The document is exactly eight pages long, a common octavo size for the folded, large printing sheets used at the time. Yet, the pages in the document were individually cut sheets. That is not just unusual, it's almost never seen. It is more likely a reflection that eight separate pages were extracted from similar books printed at the turn of the seventeenth century. That's just speculation, of course.

"The binding of loose pages tied together with a leather thong is also very unusual, even though the leather itself is definitely from the time. Why do that?"

Next, he discussed the ink.

"You had some of the ink analyzed in specialized laboratories and they reported they could not detect any chemical compounds that would be inconsistent with the claimed dates. That's true.

"However, I guess in order to totally preserve the document from damage, you only sampled the ink from the last page, which just had a stylistic printer's mark on it. That ink was legitimately old.

"I had some samples from the other pages analyzed. The first conclusion is that the ink on those pages was different from the inks on the last page. That's very unusual. How could that happen?

"Although the ink on the other pages didn't contain any detectible modern chemicals, it also didn't match any known ink profiles in the database of ancient inks, which is actually quite extensive. It's suspicious."

The type form was covered next.

"The type used and the format in the document are of a kind used around the time of Drake. However, it was extremely rare in the late 1500s, rather than even a decade or two later. Up until then, the letter "u" was not in common use; the letter "v" almost always appeared in its stead. Also, the letter "s" was written more like an "f". As its usage changed, it first appeared only as the plural designation at the end of words, not in all uses. Your document uses "u" and "s" consistently. This is very unusual, actually almost impossible to find, for the 1590s.

"The name Francis Drake appears in typescript at the end of the document. I have never seen something like that before. Why wouldn't he have signed it with pen and ink, to attest to its authenticity if nothing else?"

Jeremy continued.

"Even the fact that the document is in typeset form is hard to understand. If Drake was just leaving a record, why didn't he just write it out longhand? To get something printed secretly in Elizabethan England was difficult. The government controlled everything like that. Of course, Drake was influential and had his contacts and supporters, but why would he go to that trouble unless he wanted to make a number of copies. And yet, until now, no copy has ever surfaced or even been speculated about. That's all very unusual and not very credible. If it's real, there should be more copies."

Jeremy concluded.

"Mr. President, I know we cannot be absolute about this type of thing, but given all of those factors, I do not see any way that the Drake document could be legitimate."

Ray Cartwright had listened to Jeremy's presentation without comment or question. Jeremy was thorough and credible.

"Jeremy, thank you again. Obviously, that's not what I wanted to hear. I will just ask that you keep this totally confidential. I am determined to find out who perpetrated this fraud, but to do that we can't let anyone know that I now realize the document is a fake. That will be our secret and our leverage."

Jeremy Boucher departed and Ray Cartwright was left to contemplate what to do next. He knew that he had to do something. However, his immediate reactions were of anger and embarrassment, all mixed together.

He actually laughed out loud and said, maybe to himself, "I suspect other Presidents have gone to war or signed odious legislation without as much personal angst as I have. What a dupe! Just because I wanted something no one else had."

After a few minutes, he laughed again. "At least I didn't throw anything, or kill anyone," he mumbled. "At least, not yet."

Then his rational brain kicked in.

"Whoever did this is not going to get away with it. I can handle any personal noise or political embarrassment about this; it's only books and money. At least I could afford it.

"Wow! Who would have enough nerve to con the Vice-President of the United States like that? I need to develop a careful plan for pursuing this. Secrecy is important. If any inkling of this gets out, the culprit will disappear. He is obviously smart and tuned in.

"What secrecy? Washington has no secrets. What should I do?"

37

The next morning, after a fitful sleep, Ray Cartwright decided what his next step would be. Whatever the consequences, personally or politically, he was not going to let this go.

He called in his Executive Assistant, Elsie Browning, and asked her to locate Agent E. Z. Wilson of the FBI and, if possible, arrange a meeting with him.

Ray had held meetings with Agent Wilson in the past, when the FBI was pursuing a tax evasion scheme involving international book sellers. His name was always easy to remember for Ray, as he recalled hearing the story about how Wilson's father had named him Efrem Zimbalist Wilson, after the actor who played an FBI agent on TV decades ago. It had become a source of kidding for him when he, in fact, joined the FBI.

An hour later, she informed him that Agent Wilson would be there within the hour.

"Do you want anyone else in the meeting? Calvin Begg or Vince Larch?" referring to the President's chief of staff and general counsel.

"No. I'll just meet with Agent Wilson privately."

Elsie was a bit surprised, but said nothing more.

When Wilson arrived, the President greeted him easily, "Hello, Agent Wilson. Thank you for coming on such short notice. It's good to see you again."

"Of course, Mr. President."

"I haven't seen any messages from the Director or Administrative Assistant Director asking what this meeting is about. I'm curious; what's your internal procedure when you get a request such as I made?"

"Our protocol is laid out quite specifically. It has been in place since the days of the Watergate scandals. If any agent is approached by a senior government official, he is expected to respond privately. This allows for the possibility that the meeting might be about some wrongdoing, or at least suspicion, related to other senior government officials or Bureau personnel. It's designed to prevent inadvertent leakage of information to someone who might be involved. Once we have heard the information, we are then expected to brief more senior people in the Bureau as appropriate."

"That makes sense."

Agent Wilson then sat quietly, waiting to hear what the President was going to say.

"What I have to tell you involves a personal fraud which occurred a couple of years ago. It isn't related to the government or any officials. I purchased a very valuable antiquarian document for my personal collection that now turns out to be a fake."

Ray Cartwright then told Wilson about his dealings with Alan Page.

After hearing Ray out, Wilson said, "Let me get this straight. You paid over two million dollars for a document that you thought was a Sir Francis Drake original from the 1500s, and you now know it is fake?'

"Correct."

"Alan Page told you about this document, saying a purchase needed to be kept secret because the sellers didn't want any publicity?"

"Right."

"However, Alan Page did not actually describe the document to you in detail or represent it to be authentic. In fact, he told you that he had never seen the document?"

"Yes."

"He also said he did not know who the seller was. All of his contact had been by phone?"

"Yes."

"Alan Page didn't give you the document; it just turned up at your hotel in Vancouver."

"Yes."

"You gave Alan Page a direct commission for bringing the document to your attention, but actually paid for it by sending the rest of the money to a bank account in the Bahamas?"

"Yes."

"You had some general tests done on the document at the time, but you didn't get any expert opinions or advice until very recently?"

"Yes." Ray's responses had become quieter as the questions continued. He realized how foolish and gullible he sounded.

Ray had not told Agent Wilson anything about how he secured the money to pay for the document. That didn't seem relevant.

Wilson contemplated what he had heard.

"Well. There is no doubt that you were conned, although a good lawyer would have a field day defending the culprit, saying that no one actually represented anything fraudulent to you. Based on what you said, Alan Page seems to have covered himself off very well. And, no one else directly talked to you."

Ray hadn't thought of that reality. Basically, he had been the victim of his own collector's folly.

"Mr. President, surely you considered the possibility that the document was a forgery?"

"Certainly. But, that was one of many possibilities."

"My research indicated that totally fake documents are very unusual in the antiquarian book world. They are too difficult to create. Of course, I now know how true that is.

"Counterfeit books are more common. That is, books that are created to look like the real thing. Remember, books usually have many copies. The counterfeiting usually involves replacing missing parts, especially maps and drawings that have been removed, with ones from other publications or printed facsimiles. In this case, there was no other known reference to the document.

"As an analogy, money is counterfeited. It's a copy of something that's real, and it is used to generate real money in return for the counterfeiter. Fake Rolex watches and Gucci purses are counterfeits, as far as the legitimate manufacturers are concerned, but the actual purchasers usually know they are fake. They just want the illusion of grandeur. They aren't harmed by the transaction. True fakes, that is the creation of something that never existed in the first place but that seems to have value, are rare in the book business, unlike for antique furniture, porcelain, or even paintings.

"I also considered that the document might have been stolen. Again that seemed unlikely, since, if it had been in some major collection or in some government archive, it surely would have been revealed over the centuries and reported missing if it was taken.

"The story that Alan Page passed on about it being discovered in some private location and being sold secretly, to avoid publicity and potential confiscation, seemed quite credible."

"OK. I will need some time to decide on the next steps. I probably will want to talk with Jeremy Boucher, to see if he can give me any more information about the creation of the document. I will also want to talk with Alan Page, but that will need to be planned carefully; he has to be considered a prime suspect."

"That makes sense."

"Can I take the document and your various reports with me?"

"Of course."

"I will need to file an internal report about this, but that can be kept relatively confidential, at least for now. Of course, if we do apprehend someone, then everything will become public. As you told Boucher, keeping this quiet serves us well; we don't want the perpetrator to know that we are even aware of his existence."

Ray interjected, "I think I will directly inform the FBI Director after all. I don't want this to turn into anything inappropriate or political. It should be treated as a routine investigation."

"That's fine," Wilson replied, thinking that nothing can really be routine when it involves the President.

"Is there anything else that you need?"

"I should have the record of the bank transfer to the Bahamas. We will want to pursue that, I'm sure."

"I can get that for you; it's in my files in Seattle. When you see it, you will note that the funds were actually sent by a Seattle book dealer, Herb Trawets of Herb's Books. I was making other book purchases at the same time and Herb handled the money flow for all of them. However, Herb had no actual knowledge of the Drake document per se, and so I don't think it will be necessary for you to talk with him."

"That's fine. As I said, we want to keep knowledge of our investigation as confidential as possible."

"There is something else that comes to mind," said Ray. "In two weeks, there's a major antiquarian book fair in San Francisco, and, the following week, there's a significant book auction in Vancouver. Many of the key players in the industry who would be interested in books such as Drake's will be there, including Jeremy Boucher and Alan Page, I'm sure. Perhaps you want to observe those events before you talk to Alan."

"That could be a good idea. I will consider it."

As Agent Wilson left the President, he just shook his head and thought, "You have got to be kidding me! Someone had the nerve to cheat the President of the United States out of more than two million dollars. That takes guts."

38

Upon returning to his office, Agent Wilson set in motion two separate administrative searches for financial information.

The first was to check on Alan Page's financial status. Did he appear to have an extra two million dollars hanging about?

Asset registers, income tax filings, foreign travel records, lifestyle habits such as gambling or drugs—they were all checked. If anything, they showed Alan to be living a life of less style than expected. He truly seemed to be a bit of a freelance drifter who didn't manage his money very well.

A personal profile program, called GRINCH, was used to analyze Alan's financial position. Although the acronym stood for Gross Income Check, internally it was called Greedy Income Cheaters. Someone in the government computer services department obviously had a sense of humor.

The IRS knew very well that people tended to under-report their income if at all possible. Sure, regularly employed people had formal tax forms issued by their employers, reporting their income and the taxes withheld. But, what about free-lancing home repair services, plumbers, electricians, and painters, let alone family-run shops and restaurants, and all the serving people that received tips? Independent booksellers have the same opportunities and temptations.

The IRS assumed that most people in those positions would hide up to 25 percent of their income; usually it was more like 10 or 15 percent. GRINCH was designed to detect people who exceeded that level. It analyzed whether someone's assets and lifestyle were more extensive than what would be expected, based on their reported income.

As anyone who reads the news or sees movies knows, that's how gangsters are usually convicted. Tax evasion is the charge, not robbery, extortion, or murder.

Alan passed all the screening tests.

The next initiative was to trace the money that had been sent to the Bahamas years ago.

Decades earlier, such a search would have been impossible. The banks of the Bahamas, Cayman Islands, Switzerland, and many other places were secretive and impenetrable.

Now, however, access is much better, if somewhat bureaucratic. Driven by governments, such as the U.S., to catch citizen tax evaders, international sanctions and threats had changed the system.

Although it took a few days to obtain the information, Agent Wilson finally had a report. He was flabbergasted.

Over two million dollars had been sent to an account in the Bahamas. Meticulously, over a few months after that, the money had been distributed to dozens of other accounts, where the money was again transferred on. In an eventual myriad of transactions under $10,000, the trail stopped. That meant there were about 250 ultimate transactions!

Agent Wilson felt like he was in a Hollywood movie where such occurrences were treated as easy. He knew they were not.

"How could someone arrange all of those processes? A book dealer? Did that mean that this transaction was just a small part of something much larger? What was going on?"

At that point, he decided he needed to get some input from someone much more senior. He made an appointment with the Director of the FBI, his ultimate superior.

39

Sybil Stella Stephens was the Director of the FBI. She was a tough, no-nonsense leader.

In the world of government and political reporting, the media loved to use initials; we all know who JFK, LBJ, RFK and MLK were. The Bush presidents kind of messed that up with GHWB and GWB, but then we got used to just W. President Clinton's WJC never really caught on. After all, once he was caught fooling around with interns in the White House, he just became Bill. President Obama avoided BHO, since, in his times, a middle name of Hussein was less than ideal. Ray Cartwright, on the other hand, had fashioned his campaign around his initials. Who could forget "America: ROC Solid."

Sybil Stephens had naturally become SSS in the media, although some detractors were prone to pronounce it as a protracted hiss, rather than three distinct letters. Sometimes in conversations her name would become just Ssssss-ybil.

She was a lawyer by training, who had worked in the Justice Department for many years. She eventually became the Deputy Attorney General and then the Deputy Chief of Staff to Cartwright's predecessor, Stanley Harris, before being appointed Director of the FBI. She was a consummate Washington insider, administratively and politically.

The President had in fact called her right after his initial meeting with Agent Wilson to inform her about his problem with the fraudulent collector document. She appreciated being kept in the loop on anything that could turn political, but at that time decided to just let normal procedures unfold. Agent Wilson was quite competent.

Now, in the meeting with Wilson, she contemplated what she had just heard from him. The funds that had been sent to the Bahamas by Ray Cartwright had been laundered in a very elaborate fashion. It seemed far too sophisticated for a simple book transaction. That was worth investigating.

She didn't really care about whether Ray Cartwright had been cheated out of his money. After all, he was very rich and, based on what she had heard from Agent Wilson, he had foolishly purchased the document without adequate confirmation. What she did care about was whether or not the situation posed any security threat. Could the President be subject to personal or political blackmail over this? She would keep that possibility in mind.

She listened, with a little amusement, to Agent Wilson's thesis that a good lawyer could claim that no crime had been committed since there was no one who had actually made a false statement to President Cartwright. He had talked himself into it.

She replied, "There is fabrication and fraud here. Any jury would agree. The old homily that if it looks like a duck, walks like a duck, and quacks like a duck, it's a duck, would apply. In any case we will have money laundering and tax evasion charges."

She agreed with Wilson that he should interview Jeremy Boucher for more information before he confronted Alan Page.

40

The California Antiquarian Book Fair was being held in San Francisco this year, having been in Los Angeles the previous year. The venue was the Concourse Exhibition Center, a fifteen minute drive south of central San Francisco. The organizers made the location accessible for attendees from out of town by arranging a constant shuttle service from Union Square.

The building was a long, narrow, warehouse-like structure that stretched along a whole city block. The book dealers' booths were arranged along two aisles that seemed to stretch forever.

As had been the case in Los Angeles, the fair attracted a large number of dealers and collectors over three days.

Agent Wilson had flown in for the last two days of the fair, arriving on the Friday evening.

He had phoned Jeremy Boucher a few days earlier and explained that he was working on the fraudulent book case that involved President Cartwright. He emphasized that the investigation was still being kept very confidential and that he simply wanted to talk with Jeremy to gather more information. They had agreed to meet on Saturday morning, before the fair opened for the day.

Seated in Wilson's hotel room with room-service breakfast arranged, they met at 8:00 a.m.

"Thank you for meeting with me, Mr. Boucher," opened Wilson.

"No problem. The President told me that he was going to pursue this."

"I have talked to the President in detail, and I have read your reports on the Drake document. I have some questions."

"Sure, fire away."

"Who do you think could have created the document?"

"I have actually thought about that quite a bit since I met with the President. It seems pretty obvious that the person who created it has a lot of knowledge of the antiquarian book business.

"The content of the document reflects very detailed knowledge of the exploits of Sir Francis Drake. The style of the document shows good knowledge of old books. The paper, ink, and typeset show access to special materials.

"Even though, to an expert, the document would not stand up to careful scrutiny, as I showed, it is still quite elaborate and well done. It would have taken time and perseverance to create the final product."

"Can you be any more specific?"

"Not really. Any expert dealer with time and resources could probably do it."

"Could you have done it?"

Jeremy smiled. "Sure, but I would have done it better."

"How many others would have the ability?"

"That's very hard to say. Half of the two hundred dealers at the San Francisco fair could probably attempt it. There are thirty or more of them that specialize, at least partly, in books related to voyages of exploration. In the whole world, there are many more, especially in Europe."

"Was there anything in particular about the document that might help us narrow the search?"

"Not specifically. Perhaps the fact that eight separate, but similar, antique pages of paper were used might indicate that someone who had a large inventory of books was involved. Even that's a stretch, since anyone determined to locate numerous copies of a single book could do it with patience and determination."

"I am going to wander through the book fair to get a better sense of the business and some of the participants. Who are the major dealers I should check out?"

"You mean, who should be on your suspect list?" Jeremy said with a smile. He then gave Wilson a number of names, including Simon Katz, Margaret Thomas, Colin Mackenzie, and Graham Maltsby.

Wilson noted that the only two names he had heard before, Alan Page and Herb Trawets, were not mentioned.

When the book fair opened for business later that morning, Efrem Wilson, dressed in casual slacks and an open-necked, striped shirt, quite out of the norm for an FBI agent, paid his entry fee, picked up a catalogue, and entered the exhibition hall.

Checking the catalogue, he saw it included a map of the layout of booths and that dealers were listed alphabetically with their locations shown.

Looking around, his first impression was that the place was busy, but not bustling. The customers were well spread out through the venue. In each dealer booth area, on average, there might be one or two people browsing. There was a quiet hum of conversations, louder than a library but quieter than a shopping mall.

He wandered into many booths, avoiding the ones on Boucher's list to start with, just to get the rhythm of the place. He quickly learned that, although a dealer would approach him when he entered the booth and ask if he was looking for anything in particular, he was left alone to look around when he said he was just browsing. There were no overt sales pitches given. Dealers knew that collectors would speak up if they found something of interest.

The conversations that he overheard between dealers and collectors seemed very focused on the detailed attributes of a particular book or two. Sales didn't seem to happen often or quickly. Of course, with books priced from hundreds to many thousands of dollars, sales volume was not the main criteria.

Wilson became quite fascinated with the range of books that were available. He was surprised that he was able to pick up and browse through almost any book on display, even ones that were priced for tens of thousands of dollars.

After a while, he did purposefully search out the dealers in books related to voyages of exploration and discovery who Boucher had flagged. Other than putting some faces to the names, he didn't really learn much more. He was intrigued to see a few copies of the original publications related to the voyages of Sir Francis Drake. A first edition of the 1628 *World Encompassed* had a price tag of $250,000.

He did hear a few conversations among the dealers that related to the auction coming up in Vancouver next week. There seemed to be an undercurrent of excitement and anticipation.

He did not see anyone who looked like Alan Page. He had obtained a picture from his dealer website.

Agent Wilson's next step was going to be to meet Alan Page. He planned to do that in Vancouver next week. He had determined that Alan was going to be there by having flight plans searched. Alan was booked on a flight from Phoenix to Vancouver next Wednesday.

Wilson also wanted to observe the auction. He felt that more of the key players in the business would be there, dealers and collectors alike.

Besides, Vancouver was where the Drake document was actually delivered to President Cartwright.

41

The day of the Vancouver auction approached, preceded by two days of a public display of the collection for potential purchasers, as was normal.

The auction was planned for Thursday. BB Bookshelf Auctions had specifically chosen the date for the auction to follow the San Francisco fair by a few days, hoping that dealers and collectors from eastern North America and Europe who attended the fair would be enticed to come to Vancouver.

As a further attraction, and hopefully to stimulate more interest and excitement, they had also organized a reception for Wednesday evening at the auction venue, the Hotel Vancouver. The evening would begin with an open bar at 6:00 p.m., followed by a presentation on the history of George Vancouver, and conclude with an extensive buffet selection of appetizers and food stations, enabling everyone to mingle, but also to come and go at their own pace.

The concept of the presentation about George Vancouver had been suggested to the auction house by Jonathan Robertson, a professor of geography and history at the University of British Columbia. He specialized in the Northwest America exploration period from the late 1500s to the mid-1800s.

There had been a reasonable amount of local press coverage following the Cushing auction and the ensuing announcement of the Vancouver auction. After all, the city was named after the man.

The general gist of the local newspaper articles was that there was an outstanding collection, potentially worth millions of dollars, coming up for sale. The collection was accurately described as having been accumulated over many decades by a wealthy British Columbia industrialist who had a keen interest in local history, and the passion to find outstanding books, manuscripts, paintings, and collectible ephemera related to that history.

The articles inevitably referred to Captain George Vancouver as the famous British naval captain who fearlessly explored the Pacific west coast of America, was the first to determine that Vancouver Island was, in fact, an island, and then took possession of the region from the Spanish, who had controlled the area for the previous two hundred years. After all, this piece of history was common knowledge for every Canadian school kid.

Vancouver's Vengeance

When Jonathan read those descriptions of George Vancouver, he was frustrated. He knew that most of those characterizations were not close to being true. Canadian school books and local politicians had simplified and romanticized Vancouver's adventures over the years.

He decided to take advantage of the news coverage and, playing on the fact that few people actually knew very much about George Vancouver, he contacted BB Bookshelf Auctions. He sent a note with a bold preamble:

"Don't you think your customers would be intrigued to learn the truth about George Vancouver?"

He followed that with a simple table of information:

George Vancouver:

Legend	Reality
Naval hero	Navy and society outcast
Discoverer of Vancouver Island	The Spanish were first
Amazing explorer	Missed the Columbia River
Deposer of the Spanish	He was turned away
Admired author of journals	Published posthumously
Died as a famous explorer	Died sick and poor at 40

Come and learn the truth about this namesake historical figure!

When Gunther Shultz saw the note, he was immediately interested. He contacted Jonathan Robertson and they agreed that he would prepare a lecture about George Vancouver for the evening before the auction.

They would prominently display posters around the pre-auction venue that announced the lecture, highlighted with the same summary table that Jonathan had created to get BB Bookshelf Auctions' attention.

They also agreed that Jonathan would provide some references to the items in the auction to be held the following day.

42

Agent Wilson's attending the auction was slightly complicated by the fact that the auction was being held in Canada. He had no jurisdiction there, and he couldn't just sneak across the border on official business.

After a series of phone conversations, during which the nature of the case was described in general terms, Wilson was referred to Inspector Fleming of the Royal Canadian Mounted Police in Vancouver.

As he waited for a phone connection to be completed, Wilson recalled some of his previous experiences with the RCMP. As with many Americans, his earliest exposure to the Mounties, as everyone calls them in Canada, was seeing them in news clips where they appeared in their bright scarlet uniforms at special events such as Presidential visits to Ottawa. It took him a while to realize that the RCMP in Canada fills all of the roles of the FBI, the Secret Service, the Treasury Agents, and many other groups in the U.S. They are even called out to assist the Coast Guard if a ship has to be confronted offshore; the Canadian Coast Guard is not armed! As well, the Mounties provide police services for many of the Canadian provinces. Being pulled over for speeding on a British Columbia highway by a Mountie surprises many American tourists. It's never a good idea, at times like that, to suggest that the officer could better spend his time chasing spies or catching real criminals.

"Inspector Fleming, it's a pleasure to talk with you. I believe that you have heard a bit about my planned trip to Vancouver from your headquarters. Simply put, I want to observe the book auction that's about to take place there, and I want to make contact with one or two people who will be attending it, all Americans. I would appreciate your assistance."

"That will be no problem, Agent Wilson. Yes, I have been briefed."

"The auction begins at 11:00 a.m. on Thursday. I plan to fly to Vancouver on Wednesday. Perhaps we could meet ahead of the event, Wednesday evening or Thursday morning?"

"Let me know your flight plans and where you are staying and I will have someone meet you at the airport, and then we can get together for dinner on Wednesday. Travelling from the east, you will undoubtedly get here in the afternoon, with our three-hour time zone shift."

"Thank you. I'll see you then."

At four Wednesday afternoon, Efrem Wilson landed at the Vancouver International airport after a five-hour flight from Washington. An RCMP officer, dressed in a working-day blue uniform met him and drove him to his hotel in a dark, unmarked sedan. He was staying at the Pender Howe Inn, an older, established hotel a few blocks from the site of tomorrow's auction. Although he didn't actually know any of the book dealers, and they certainly wouldn't know him, he wanted to minimize the chance of any random encounters. It was unlikely; Vancouver is a large, bustling city.

He had the good humor to say to his escort, "I guess scarlet serge and limousines are reserved for real dignitaries."

She replied with a straight face, "I guess they're dignitaries, mostly politicians."

He laughed.

At six he met Inspector Fleming in the lobby of his hotel and they headed into the dining room.

"I'm sure this is a bit early for you, Inspector, but it is nine eastern time. I appreciate that."

They exchanged business cards. Having passed over his Efrem Z. Wilson identification, he was a little amused to read Ian L. Fleming, Inspector on the other card.

Although he wasn't certain that the RCMP Inspector would be informal enough with him, he ventured, "Do you ever get addressed as Bond?"

Inspector Fleming laughed and they went on to share their personal stories and angst about their names and experiences at the police academies.

Over dinner, Wilson shared the general outline of his mission.

"A fake antiquarian book was sold for a large sum of money, millions. I want to observe some of the major players in that world of valuable books related to ancient explorers. Many of them will be at tomorrow's auction.

"Afterwards, I want to arrange a meeting with one of the book dealers, Alan Page from Phoenix. He might be able to shed some light on the deal.

"I would like you to accompany me to the auction and share your impressions. Also, since I have no status here, perhaps you could approach Mr. Page and ask him to meet with me?"

Inspector Ian Fleming totally understood that Agent Efrem Wilson had given him a sanitized version of his mission. Special Agents of the FBI, based in Washington, D.C., don't fly to Vancouver to casually chat with a book dealer who lives in Arizona. He accepted the omissions as just par for the course in international policing.

"It should be interesting. What if we meet here for breakfast at nine in the morning and then walk over to the auction. It's only ten minutes away."

43

At the same time that Agent Wilson and Inspector Fleming were having dinner a few blocks away, BB Bookshelf Auctions' opening reception got underway.

Gunther Shultz was pleased to see a large group of people wander in. He recognized many major book dealers and collectors. He guessed that the offer of free drinks and food, even if it included a lecture by a university professor, attracted everyone.

Of course, the general chatter was about tomorrow's auction.

At six thirty, everyone filed into a large hotel meeting room set up with rows of chairs in front of a lecture podium. Easels were set up on either side of the podium and an overhead-projection screen hung from the ceiling.

Waiters made sure that everyone had a glass in hand as they entered.

Jonathan, standing at the lectern, epitomized a history professor. Of medium height and slim, in his early fifties, he was dressed in a tweed jacket, complete with leather elbow patches, over plain slacks, with a light-colored, patterned, long-sleeved shirt, and a pale wool tartan tie. He even had a neatly trimmed beard.

"Welcome, everyone. We're so pleased that you have taken the time to join us for the evening. Over the next hour, I hope to educate and enlighten you about George Vancouver, the central figure in tomorrow's exciting auction. We will take a short break partway through, so that the waiters can refill your glasses."

There was a short burst of laughter at that, possibly out of relief. After all, they were going to be sitting through a lecture by a history professor.

"I know you saw the poster outside, challenging your perception of George Vancouver. Hopefully, an hour from now, you will appreciate why I posted those comments. Let's start:

"It is London, 1772. Captain James Cook had returned from his first historic voyage around the world a year earlier. He was about to embark on a second voyage to explore the South Pacific and search for a new southern continent.

Vancouver's Vengeance

"George Vancouver was ecstatic. He had been chosen to sail with Captain James Cook on that second voyage. He was fourteen years old.

"In the first session this evening, I will discuss George Vancouver's background and experiences over the ensuing twenty years, which led to his being chosen to lead his own historic expedition, and I will examine the details of the Vancouver expedition itself. The second session, after our short break, will cover the aftermath and legacy of Vancouver's voyage.

"George Vancouver was born in 1757 in the North Sea port city of King's Lynn. His father, John Joseph Vancouver, was a prestigious, reasonably well-off merchant class member, who had served in public roles such as sheriff and customs collector. Although definitely not part of the aristocratic upper class, he was reasonably well connected.

"The second half of the eighteenth century was a time of exploration and discovery. Perhaps two dozen voyages around the world had occurred in the previous two hundred and fifty years, since the time of Magellan and Drake. Most of those were voyages of trade to Spanish America and the Far East. There had been little deviation in routes from the mid-latitudes, dictated by the prevailing trade winds.

"Cook's first voyage, from 1769 to 1771, had explored new lands. He discovered New Zealand, surveyed the eastern coast of Australia, and encountered many new tribes and cultures on dozens of newly-found Pacific islands. Joseph Banks, the famed naturalist on the voyage, returned with specimens of many new plants and animals and drawings of the far-off exotic places.

"As Cook prepared to set out on his second voyage, to further explore the Pacific and to explicitly look for a legendary, never-seen southern continent, public interest was high. The desire to be part of the voyage was rampant among seamen.

"Somehow, probably through his father's connections, George Vancouver was selected as a junior midshipman, effectively a general seaman with extra status as a future officer in training. Such sailors were often referred to as young gentlemen. These were hard-working roles but, in the British Navy tradition, a necessary step lasting at least six years before becoming an actual officer.

"The voyage lasted three years, circumnavigating the globe at southern latitudes between 55°S and 60°S, the equivalent of southern Alaska in the northern hemisphere. Their southern-most penetration was to 71°S, where they were driven back by cold temperatures, fog, ice, and storms. There was no southern continent to be found that would be hospitable to settlement.

Vancouver's Vengeance

"A frequently-told anecdote about George Vancouver is that, when James Cook ordered his ships to turn back from their southern quest, Vancouver ran to the forward prow and screamed out "ne plus ultra," or "no one farther," meaning that he had personally gone farther south than anyone else in history. This is an amusing story that would seem to reflect the joyful exuberance of the young sailor. It is also noteworthy that there doesn't seem to be any other story about Vancouver being joyful or spontaneous at any other time in his life, a reflection of his future discipline and privacy.

"The expedition returned to a welcoming and celebratory Britain in 1775.

"In 1776 Cook headed out again, this time to explore the Pacific coast of North America. Was there truly a passage across the continent from the Atlantic to the Pacific? Legend and fanciful maps had predicted large rivers and lakes that would transverse the continent eastward from the Pacific, connecting to Hudson Bay or the Great Lakes, but they had never been found. If such a route existed, it would change the travel and trade patterns of the world between Europe and the Far East.

"It is often surprising to realize that almost three hundred years after Columbus discovered America, European explorers had not ventured up the Pacific coast of North America past California. Perhaps Sir Francis Drake had gone there in the late 1500s, and a few Spanish ships had ventured north once in a while, but there had been no organized or recorded exploration of the region. Also, no one had yet crossed North America by land.

"George Vancouver was again on the expedition, still as a junior midshipman, but assigned more senior responsibilities. This provided him with extensive experience in navigation and charting, skills that would become his personal expertise.

"The voyage was extensive. Rounding the Cape of Africa, they crossed the Indian Ocean and entered the Pacific, with stops at places such as Tahiti. Perhaps most noteworthy during the early part of the voyage, they discovered Hawaii. The Hawaiians, having never seen outsiders before, received them cordially, almost as gods. Food, supplies, and hospitality were a welcome respite for the sailors.

"Life on a navy ship in the 1700s was very tough. Cook had almost two hundred people on two ships, each about one hundred feet long, taking a voyage that would last five years! Discipline and sanitation were the obvious big issues—the first being strong and the second weak.

"For the times, James Cook was an enlightened captain. While maintaining discipline, he showed some reasonable tolerance and flexibility. This was not easy, or normal, in the British navy of the day, with the complex social strata of officers, gentlemen, and common sailors, all confined in small spaces far from home. Rules, structure, and control were important.

"Vancouver and fellow junior ranks, such as William Bligh, observed and admired Cook's methods, but, as time would show, they did not learn them very well.

"In March, 1778, almost two years after leaving England, Cook's ships reached the northwest coast of America, north of Spanish California in today's Oregon.

"The weather was poor, with rain and fog. Although they were ostensibly searching for possible transcontinental passages, they passed by both the Columbia River and the Strait of Juan de Fuca without detecting them.

"Finally, on the outer coast of Vancouver Island, which they did not recognize as an island, they found Nootka Sound. That place became their base for repairs and replenishing, as well as their main point of contact with the local natives. Over the next two decades, this harbor would become one of the most important on the Pacific, almost causing a major war between Britain and Spain.

"The natives at Nootka were friendly and hospitable. Their villages were substantial, with sturdy wooden homes and decorative trappings such as totem poles; they travelled in large wooden canoes; and their social interactions involved music, dancing, and lavish feasts. Cook felt welcome.

"They exchanged gifts and traded for supplies. Metal objects of any kind—nails to cooking pots—were prized by the natives. Beyond supplies, the sailors traded for sea otter pelts, which, as it turned out, would be the commodity that changed the region forever.

"Cook, and Britain for many years after, believed that he was the first European to sail these waters and to discover the coastal areas. They were wrong. Spanish naval captains such as Perez and Quadra had been here years earlier. However, the Spanish treated all such information as a military and national secret. Unlike the British, they didn't publish their naval journals for the world to read.

"Cook then sailed farther north, reaching the Aleutians and a large inlet near 60°N, now called Cook Inlet. They were turned back by cold weather and ice, just as they had been at similar southern latitudes on the previous voyage. Cook concluded that there was no passage south of the Arctic across North America, although his lack of detailed surveying would leave the subject open to debate for many more years, that is, until Vancouver returned in the 1790s.

"Cook then headed back to Hawaii to wait out the winter. Again, he was well received when he reached Hawaii. However, after once departing he again returned due to a broken mast. The mood had changed. The natives became hostile and attacked the landing party, killing Cook. The change in attitude has never been fully explained. Speculation is that Cook had worn out his welcome by violating some of the religious traditions and legends of the tribes.

"Vancouver observed all of this and was part of the ship's crew that futilely attempted to rescue Cook.

"If you momentarily turn your attention to the two easels on my far right and to the overhead screen, you will see the two most famous illustrations of the confrontation between Cook's sailors and the natives. The first is by George Carter and the second is by John Webber. They certainly capture the intense emotion of the event. As you all know, they are part of the auction offering tomorrow.

"There is a grisly side to the story that needs telling, as it provides a contrast for Vancouver's later return to Hawaii. After Cook was killed, Vancouver negotiated for the return of his body. However, it had been cut up and shared among many tribe chieftains; parts were cooked and eaten. All that was eventually returned were a few disparate body parts.

"Under the command of the next most senior officer, Charles Clerke, the ships then returned to Alaska for another attempt to discover a northern passage, this time through the Bering Strait into the Arctic Ocean. Again, they were turned back by the elements. They then returned to Britain via China.

"During their stopover in Canton, they were astonished to discover how valuable their sea otter furs were in trade for silks, spices, and teas. What they had obtained from the natives for minor metal objects, converted to Oriental commodities, resulted in significant wealth when they reached home.

"Almost immediately after returning to Britain in late 1780, George Vancouver, now a twenty-three year old with eight years of seafaring experience, was promoted to lieutenant, a full-fledged officer.

"Over the next ten years he served on various navy ships. He had duty patrolling the North Sea and the Caribbean, experiencing one actual naval battle with the Spanish, and conducting surveys of coasts and harbors in Jamaica.

The Death of Captain James Cook by the Indians of O.Whyee (1779) by George Carter, 1784

"The navy life on these assignments was quite different than it had been on the Cook exploration expeditions. Discipline was harsh, ship conditions were much worse, and little time was spent relaxing or socializing in ports. Vancouver became a somewhat-hardened leader.

"In late 1789, having performed well, he was promoted to be second in command of a ship, *Discovery*, that was being readied for another voyage of exploration to the south Pacific. However, world events would change those plans and firmly position Vancouver for the history books.

"A lot had happened in the north Pacific off America during the ten years since Cook's last voyage. There were two converging, but competing, phenomena.

"First, the Spanish had stepped up their long-held claim that the entire Pacific coast, north to Russian Alaska, was their territory. This was triggered by the publication of Cook's journals and the increased demands from other nations that Spanish claims of unsettled territories were invalid. These other nations said that those areas, such as the north Pacific, should be considered open seas and free-trade areas,.

"The Spanish had lightly explored the region before Cook, but had not set up any permanent settlements, nor even published their activities. Now they demanded that foreign ships, such as those from Britain, stay away and refrain from trading with the natives.

"However, because of the lucrative sea otter trade that Cook's voyage had identified, by the late 1780s there were many ships in the region in any year—as many as two dozen at a time from Spain, France, Portugal, Britain, and the United States.

"It is quite amazing that few sailors were lost on these many long voyages far from home. One notable exception was the loss of over twenty men from the voyage of the famous French explorer La Perouse. While surveying a coastal inlet near Alaska, their longboat was trapped in a violent clash of waves and tides and was dashed on the protruding rocks. This dramatic event is vividly captured in the painting by Louis Crepin which is mounted on the third easel and is now being projected overhead.

"To avoid directly antagonizing the Spanish, British trading ships often cloaked their true identity in a facade of Portuguese registration. This also allowed them to ignore the British-created monopoly, the British East India Company, which had been established to license and regulate British trading in the Pacific.

The Death of Captain James Cook (1779) by John Webber, 1785

"One such British trader was John Meares, who, in a Portuguese-registered ship, traded with the natives for sea otter pelts in 1786. Apparently trying to get an early start on the 1787 season, he decided to overwinter on the coast, rather than retreat to Hawaii as was the custom for all other traders. As a result, most of his crew died due to the weather and scurvy, another sad experience. A handful of the sailors, including Meares, were rescued by another British trader, George Dixon.

"This led to a bitter controversy between the two men. Dixon, who was registered with the East India Company, demanded that Meares, who was not, promise not to return. Meares, on the other hand, sued Dixon for charging him too much for the rescue.

"In any case, Meares returned to Nootka in 1788, where he did build a small structure to use as a base for his trading operations. He also assembled a small trading vessel that he had brought from China. These settlement activities were to later create a major international incident.

"The next year, 1789, Meares formed a private trading company in China and sent four ships to Nootka. The leader of the expedition was James Colnett.

"At the same time, the Spanish, spurred on by the increased trading in the area and the encroaching Russian presence, decided to establish a permanent settlement at Nootka. They sent a commander, Esteban Martinez, with a small military force to assert Spain's sovereignty in the region and to prevent other countries from trading with the natives.

"When Martinez arrived in Nootka in May, 1789, he found many European ships present, all trading for sea otter pelts. He confronted these operations, expelling some and seizing others. Among those he seized were the British ships of Meares's company and, in particular, the ship *Argonaut* captained by Colnett.

"At this time, Britain and Spain were in the midst of many disputes and counter-claims, mostly arising out of their different positions on controlled territories versus open seas. However, they were not at war.

"It was in that context that the British were preparing their navy ship *Discovery*, with Vancouver as second-in-command, to head to the Pacific and establish some sort of presence, thus confronting the Spanish, and to again search for the possible northwest passage between 51°N and 60°N. They were not convinced that Cook's exploration had been definitive enough.

"However, in April, 1790, John Meares arrived in Britain with the tales of his ships being seized by the Spanish and with exaggerated claims about his settlements, deals with the natives, and trading activities.

The Shipwreck of LaPerouse's Yawl, Port Francis, Alaska (1786) by Louis Crepin, 1800

"This created a furor in Britain. Spurred by the British sense of international importance since the voyages of Cook and the outcries of the wealthy investment and trading groups, who were making large profits in foreign trade, Britain confronted Spain.

"The press inflamed the issues in stories and editorials, including a graphic illustration of the Spanish seizing Colnett's ship at Nootka labelled "*The Spanish Insult to the British Flag at Nootka Sound*," never mentioning that the ship was actually sailing under a Portuguese flag. That very detailed image by Robert Dodd is mounted on the easel immediately to my left. This is an image that almost started a war; Britain and Spain were the two most powerful nations at that time.

A conflict would inevitably draw in France, the Netherlands, the new United States, and many other countries.

"Britain mobilized its navy. Spain sent reinforcements to its outposts. Diplomatic demands and threats were made. The countries prepared for war. In that context, Vancouver was reassigned to a war ship.

"Finally, cooler heads in government prevailed and a treaty was signed, the Nootka Sound Convention. Its key element was to declare that all areas north of lands already settled by the Spanish on the American Pacific coast were to be considered free trade regions with open ports.

"Britain decided to renew the planned trip of the *Discovery*, this time with the added mandate to recover the seized British lands at Nootka. Since the original captain for that voyage had been reassigned during the war preparations, George Vancouver now returned to the ship as its commander.

"He was given many assignments for the voyage by the Admiralty, some of them ambiguous, and some contradictory. Generally, he was to:

- Acquire detailed knowledge of the northwest coast of America from 30°N (California) to 60°N (Alaska).
- Identify any significant waterways that could lead to the interior by ship, portending a possible Northwest Passage.
- Locate the fabled Strait of Anian, near the latitude 48°N.
- Locate all European settlements, particularly Spanish ones, on the Pacific coasts of America, and determine when they had been founded.
- Determine the northern extent of Spanish occupation and, thus, the southern border of the free trade region.
- Survey Hawaii during the winter months.
- Reclaim Meares's British lands, ships, and buildings at Nootka.

The Spanish Insult to the British Flag at Nootka Sound (1789) by Robert Dodd, 1791

"That's quite an amazing list.

"Vancouver commanded two ships, the *Discovery* and the *Chatham*. The former was 330 tons, 100 feet in length, and had a complement of one hundred men. The latter was only 130 tons, 53 feet long, and held forty-five sailors. Together they set sail on April 1, 1791 for a four-and-a-half year voyage of adventure.

"Here, I will divert to describe three members of the ships' complement who were destined to play a critical role in George Vancouver's destiny.

"The first was Archibald Menzies, a botanist-naturalist-surgeon. His early naval career included assignments in Canada. He had also sailed with Colnett in his early Pacific voyages to Nootka and Hawaii. He had become a protégé of Joseph Banks, the naturalist who had sailed with Cook on his first voyage. Banks was a very influential aristocrat in British social and political circles. For reasons that are not totally clear, but perhaps due to perceived differences in social status and lack of due deference by the navy men, Banks had become distant from Cook after his first voyage and he had developed a poor relationship with Vancouver. Banks had Menzies assigned to Vancouver's voyage as the botanist-naturalist, reporting back to himself in London, not to the voyage commander. This obviously irritated Vancouver.

"Vancouver and Menzies were destined to clash often over the years ahead.

"The second individual was a young aristocrat, Thomas Pitt, who joined the voyage as a midshipman, or young gentleman, over the objections of Vancouver. It was done at the insistence of Pitt's father, the influential Lord Camelford. Young Pitt was also the nephew of the Prime Minister, William Pitt, and of the First Lord of the Admiralty, John Pitt, the Earl of Chatham. Thomas Pitt was impetuous, prone to disobedience and anger, and had little respect for Vancouver or his authority. It was a recipe for disaster.

"The third critical person was Vancouver himself.

"Recall that he was the son of a merchant-class family, who went to sea at the age of fourteen. Although he had progressed well in the navy and had developed key skills in navigation and charting, he had little formal educational training or leadership skills.

"In his youth, he had observed the somewhat open style of James Cook, but as an officer he had experienced the more formal, restrained style of the mainline navy. Due to his inexperience, and probable insecurity, he developed a by-the-book command discipline.

"He also had little experience or comfort in dealing with aristocrats and politicians, such as Joseph Banks and Lord Camelford. His reaction was to resent their interference in his naval responsibilities, which they interpreted as inappropriate disrespect.

"On top of all that, he was not a well person, even at the age of thirty-four. He was often physically sick and weak, and he suffered bouts of anxiety and uncontrolled anger. It is not clear what ailed him, but more recent interpretations of his symptoms suggest he suffered from chronic kidney disease, perhaps due to exposure to malaria early in his career.

"All of these limitations would play out with consequence.

"The first year of the voyage saw the ships sail down the Atlantic, pass south of the Cape of Africa, survey New Zealand and eastern Australia, visit various Pacific islands, and finally reach the California coast in April, 1792.

"There were a number of incidents over that first year that set the tone for the whole voyage.

"Vancouver had a number of confrontations with Menzies over their roles, the maintenance of Menzies's botanical samples on the ship, and priorities at various ports of call. Menzies would dispatch critical reports back to Joseph Banks in London at every opportunity.

"Vancouver dispensed harsh discipline to his crew for violations large and small; the lash was used often and brutally.

"Thomas Pitt committed numerous acts of sullen disobedience and insubordination. Vancouver had Pitt flogged, an almost unheard of thing involving a young gentleman, let alone one of an aristocratic family.

"Even after many months at sea in the small, often-fetid ships, Vancouver would not allow the crew to disembark in stops such as Tahiti. He was aware that Captain Bligh had suffered a mutiny from his crew, who refused to return to the ship after an extended stay a few years earlier. Vancouver was not going to take any chances.

"Vancouver's harshness, periods of irrational anger, and inconsistency alienated his officers who, after a few months at sea, even refused to dine with him onboard.

"It was not a band of happy adventurers who arrived in America.

"Vancouver and his crew then commenced their detailed survey of the west coast of North America north of California. That task would consume much of the next three summer seasons. Whatever else came from Vancouver's voyage, this would be its defining achievement.

"The routine of the surveys would typically have the two major ships anchor in some sheltered position. Then crews of fifteen or twenty sailors would set out in smaller boats for about ten days at a time, meticulously surveying every bay, inlet, and island they encountered. The officers would survey and take positional readings as the crew rowed and manipulated small sails. They would eventually travel over 10,000 miles in those boats as they surveyed 1,700 miles of coastline.

"Off the coast of today's Washington State (everything north of California was generally referred to as Oregon at the time), Vancouver met up with an American trader-explorer, Robert Gray. In this period, after the American Revolution, the United States was extending its area of interest westward.

"Vancouver and Gray shared experiences. Gray mentioned the major river to the south that he had named the Columbia. This chagrined Vancouver, as he had dismissed the apparent river opening as insignificant due to the imposing sandbar at its entrance. That was not a good start on his search for major rivers that could lead inland. Later, he would also miss the Fraser and the Skeena, large rivers that penetrate hundreds of miles inland.

"Gray confirmed that a major inland sea, the Strait of Juan de Fuca, lay ahead. This was the legendary Strait of Anian from Drake's time. He also said that he had heard stories that the lands north of that were actually a large island, but he had not confirmed that himself.

"Vancouver sailed on, surveying the Strait of Juan de Fuca, Puget Sound, and the Strait of Georgia, finally traversing the inside passage behind the large island. At the time, he believed that he was the first explorer to determine this. However, he later encountered the Spaniards Galiano and Valdes who showed they had done so earlier, even though their surveys were nowhere as detailed as Vancouver's.

"During this period Thomas Pitt was flogged twice more.

"Along the Pacific coast Vancouver encountered many different native tribes and villages. Most meetings were friendly and involved some degree of trading; recall that European traders had been in the general area for over ten years now. It is worth noting, however, that neither the tribes nor villages were ever noted on Vancouver's detailed maps. They just didn't matter to his mission or his European mentality of discovering new, open lands.

"Finally, after surveying some distance north of the island, Vancouver headed to Nootka Sound and his rendezvous with the Spanish.

Vancouver's Vengeance

"Vancouver's first impression of Nootka in August, 1792, must have been a surprise.

"During his first visit with Cook in 1778, Nootka was an undeveloped harbor with some native villages in the area. In the intervening period, he knew, it had become a base for ships to repair, replenish, and trade. Now he saw a well-established community.

"He was welcomed by the Spanish commander, Juan Francisco de la Bodega y Quadra.

"Quadra was a Peruvian-born Spanish aristocrat, well-educated, and very experienced in exploration, leadership, and diplomacy. He had arrived at Nootka six months earlier, in anticipation of Vancouver's arrival, to execute the terms of the Nootka Sound Convention between Spain and Britain.

"He had prepared the settlement well, to emphasize the area's Spanish roots. He had made the ships of all nations welcome, in the spirit of the new free trade status. He had also thoroughly researched all of the history of the area, talking to traders and native leaders. He well knew that Meares's claims were false.

"He even knew that Cook's claim of primacy in discovering the area in 1778 was false, since he had personally been there earlier.

"Vancouver was badly prepared to deal with Quadra. He only had the general instructions he received at the start of his voyage the previous year. He had expected to receive further instructions via a British supply ship that met up with him here, but the ship's captain had nothing more for him.

"The early interactions between Vancouver and Quadra were very cordial, involving many dinners, ceremonies, and visits with native leaders.

"Finally, when they came to discuss the terms of the Convention, Quadra proposed that the northern limit of established Spanish presence was the Strait of Juan de Fuca. He also stated that Meares had only occupied a small lot in the harbor; there was nothing else for the British to claim.

"None of this aligned with Vancouver's expectations. He had presumed that the northern limit of true Spanish occupation was California. Although this was in fact true, Vancouver had no way to positively assert that, but had no authority to agree to anything else.

"Thus, although Vancouver and Quadra interacted very well personally, nothing was achieved. Over the next two years, as Vancouver continued his northern exploration and made winter survey trips to California and Hawaii, he awaited further instructions from home. He even sent two senior officers back to Britain—Zachary Mudge on a trader ship via China and William Broughton with Spanish assistance across Panama and the Atlantic. He never received any more information or instructions.

"One sidebar that shows the positive relationship the two men developed is that Vancouver named the large island he had charted Quadra's and Vancouver's Island. It was many years later when it was shortened to just Vancouver Island by the British.

"Over those next two years, Vancouver did have some notable achievements. He completed the detailed Pacific survey north to Cook Inlet at 60°N, finally determining that a navigable transcontinental waterway south of the Arctic did not exist.

"There is a minor historical footnote to mention here. Just a few weeks after George Vancouver surveyed the coastline slightly north of Vancouver Island, in July, 1793, Alexander Mackenzie arrived at exactly the same spot, having travelled overland. Mackenzie was the first person to cross North America by land north of Mexico. He was also searching for a water passage across the continent. Three years earlier he had been diverted to the Arctic on a similar journey, having followed the large river that now bears his name. The Lewis and Clark transcontinental journey that culminated at the mouth of the Columbia River was still more than a decade away.

"On his three visits to Hawaii, he was able to re-establish relationships with the natives, broker a peace between the various island tribes, survey the coastlines, and negotiate a protectorate-type treaty between Hawaii and Britain. This never materialized into a lasting relationship due to neglect by Britain. Eventually, after a civil war and a virtual invasion by American industrialists, it became part of the U.S.

"On board the ships, little changed. Vancouver's relationship with Menzies remained strained. Pitt continued to misbehave. He was first demoted, and then flogged again. Finally, in California in early 1794 Vancouver sent Pitt away to Australia, leaving him to fend for himself to get back to Britain.

"When the Alaska survey was completed in August, 1794, Vancouver set sail for home, continuing to scout along the way for information about Spanish settlements in Central and South America.

"By mid-1795 he had sailed around the Horn of South America and reached the island of St. Helena in the South Atlantic.

"There, as was the custom in the navy, he gathered all of the journals, logs, and drawings that had been made by everyone on the voyage. Once they were vetted by the navy back in Britain, they would usually be returned to the authors for their own use and possible commercial publication.

"Menzies did not turn in his journals, since he claimed he was there on the sponsorship of Joseph Banks, not the navy.

"At this point Vancouver also became aware of recent European developments, including the fact that Britain was at war with Napoleonic France and that many other nations were becoming involved.

"By happenstance, he encountered a Dutch East India trading ship, the *Macassar*, laden with valuables on its way to France. He seized this as a prize of war and sailed it back to Britain alongside the *Discovery*.

"The *Chatham* was diverted to Brazil to communicate orders from the Governor in St. Helena to British forces there before it returned to Britain.

"Although the seizing of the *Macassar* was a fortunate event, it caused another major problem with Menzies. Due to a shortage of crew to handle both ships and the stormy weather they encountered, the crew member who was assigned to monitor Menzies's plant enclosure on the upper deck was diverted to other duties. Most of Menzies's specimens were ruined.

"Menzies reacted in a fury, so strongly that Vancouver had him arrested and placed in irons, to await a court-martial in Britain.

"Finally, after more than four years at sea, Vancouver returned to London in October, 1795.

"That concludes our first session. After our break, I will cover Vancouver's arrival back in Britain and dissect his enduring legacy."

44

During the short break conversations were brief.

"This is far more interesting than I had expected."

"I didn't realize that George Vancouver's voyage was so complicated."

"I always thought that he discovered the island and took possession of it from the Spanish."

"Boy, he was a tough captain."

"He sure didn't show much leadership, did he?"

After everyone's drinks were refreshed, Jonathan started the second session.

"We left George Vancouver arriving home to Britain in late 1795 after more than four years at sea, having endured many hardships and disappointments along with his successful exploration and mapping exploits.

"The immediate reaction to Vancouver's return home was . . . nothing!

"The press and the public ignored his return. Compared to the welcome that Cook had received after his voyages, this was undoubtedly a huge surprise and very frustrating for Vancouver.

"However, the Spanish war threat of five years earlier had passed into memory; the current focus was on the war with France. People and the press had forgotten, or didn't care anymore, about the Spanish crisis of years past, and didn't really remember Vancouver's purpose.

"Sure, Vancouver had returned with some maps that were of interest to the navy, but all of the places he visited had been described previously by the various explorers and traders before him.

"He had not resolved any territorial issues with the Spanish, and no one seemed very interested in Hawaii, with Europe at war.

"On top of all that, official Britain was disappointed with Vancouver, even hostile.

"Over the previous two years, following the messages they received from him and the distractions of new hostilities in Europe, the British and Spanish governments had negotiated an extension to the Nootka Sound Convention. In January, 1794, they had declared the Pacific north of California to be a free trade area where no claims of sovereignty would be allowed. They also declared Nootka to be a free port, and decided to withdraw any European presence there, returning it to the natives.

"By the time Vancouver left Nootka in the summer of 1794, British and Spanish naval ships were already on the way to dismantle the settlement.

"The Admiralty had never sent any follow-up instructions to Vancouver over the years; they had not even bothered to inform him of those intervening events. Talk about being ignored, even ostracized!

"Joseph Banks mounted a campaign of criticism and censure against Vancouver. Based on Menzies's reports and his own biases, he effectively had the court martial initiated against Menzies by Vancouver dismissed. He tried to convince Menzies to publish his journals before Vancouver, but Menzies could not be bothered; he moved on to other expeditions. After all, he was primarily a scientist.

"The Thomas Pitt situation became much more serious.

"Unbeknownst to Pitt, or anyone else in the western hemisphere at the time, Pitt's father had died in January, 1793. Thus, he was then the new Lord Camelford and one of the wealthiest people in England. Oops!

"However, that remained unknown to him for a long time. More than a year after that date, having already sailed with the Vancouver expedition for two years, and having been whipped numerous times, he was dumped on a trade ship in California, headed for Australia.

"After arriving in Australia, he managed to get himself to India via various vessels. There, he signed onto a British navy ship as a lieutenant, an actual officer! Obviously, there were no ready reference checks or timely communications to Australia or India in 1794.

"Then, a year later, having left the navy in Calcutta, he learned the news of his father's death and his new position as Lord Camelford. Now being a rich man, he bought a ship. It was a poor investment; it sunk shortly afterwards in Ceylon.

"Pitt finally arrived in London in early 1796. He was about to make life very difficult for Vancouver.

"Vancouver had returned to England six months earlier. After arranging the administrative details regarding the ship and his crew, he moved to Petersham, outside London. Although still very sick, he started to compile his journals for publication, aided by his brother, John.

"Amazingly, having been at sea for almost five years and not having been paid by the navy since 1790, he wouldn't be paid anything until 1798. The establishment definitely was not on his side; quite the opposite.

"Similarly, his share of the bounty for having captured the supply ship *Macassar* in 1795 was also delayed until 1798.

"Throughout 1796 he was constantly accosted by Thomas Pitt, physically and politically. Pitt actually once went to Vancouver's home to challenge the weak, sick captain to a duel, which Vancouver managed to avoid.

"On a trip to London to visit publishers and lawyers, accompanied by his brother, he was aggressively confronted by Pitt on Conduit Street. John managed to deflect the attack. Subsequently, they obtained a legal restraining order against Pitt.

"However, the incident became public and, inflamed by Pitt and probably Banks, turned into a disaster for Vancouver. A published political cartoon in the London newspaper depicted the confrontation, labeled *The Caneing on Conduit Street.*

"This image is mounted on the last easel to my left and is also now being projected.

"It shows Vancouver as a pudgy, flamboyantly-dressed naval officer, hiding behind his brother as he is accosted by Pitt. It is the various captions that were damning: they referenced the trampling and imprisoning of crew and gentlemen, illegal sea otter trade by a naval officer, the withholding of gifts from native chiefs meant for the king, and general lying and cheating. It was vicious in its attack on Vancouver.

"Vancouver worked on compiling his journals and organizing the charts and illustrations for publication throughout 1797 and into 1798. At the end, due to his weakness, he was dictating recollections to his brother.

"Perhaps nothing better captures George Vancouver's situation and state of mind better than a letter he wrote in January, 1798. It was sent to his agent and sponsor, James Sykes. It poignantly captures the sad state of his health and finances. He laments about the disagreeable attitude of his creditors and asks for money to pay his housekeeper and to buy household supplies in anticipation of his future naval payments and the revenues from the ultimate publication of his journals. He even asks Sykes to send him some tea.

"Finally, a couple of months later, he did receive his back pay and the reward for the capture of the *Macassar*.

"However, very shortly thereafter, on May 12, 1798, Captain George Vancouver died at the age of forty.

"His brother finished compiling the last one hundred pages of the journals and oversaw their publication later that year.

"The most enduring legacy of George Vancouver is that publication, especially his detailed charts of the Pacific coast of America.

The Caneing on Conduit Street (1796), by John Gillray

"This final sequence also explains how the proof copies of the publication volumes, which are the crowning centerpiece of tomorrow's auction, are only partially signed by George Vancouver.

"And so, what have we learned about George Vancouver and his achievements?

"He certainly sailed the world extensively and was meticulous in his descriptions and charting of everything he saw. His maps of Pacific North America and Hawaii were the definitive references for a long time.

"He performed well in the first two decades of his naval career as he was learning and carrying out orders and operations under the general direction of more senior officers.

"His limited leadership experience had not prepared him well for commanding the five-year, multidimensional mandate of his Pacific voyage.

"His apparent insecurity caused him to command his ships by the book, and with harsh adherence to the rules. His officers and crew came to totally distrust and dislike him.

"His background and experiences at sea from the age of fourteen also had not prepared him for dealing with the social and political realities at senior levels. He suffered serious consequences from the conflicts with Banks, Menzies, and Pitt.

"He was ill-prepared to deal with the Spanish at Nootka and thus achieved nothing there.

"The fact that the Admiralty never sent him any further instructions, nor even informed him of the eventual disposition of Nootka, showed that they had totally lost confidence in him. They truly left him out to dry.

"However, it must be conceded that much of the public criticism that was directed at Vancouver, such as the *Caneing on Conduit Street* cartoon, was really directed at the whole British navy and its practices at the time. The public was demanding change in their harsh practices. Vancouver was a convenient symbol of that.

"It is somewhat surprising to learn that no one wrote a biography of George Vancouver until 1930, well over a hundred years after his death.

"The only portrait that has been used to depict him over the years cannot be verified. The National Portrait Gallery in London now says it is the portrait of an unknown naval captain, by an unknown artist from the eighteenth century, once attributed to being of George Vancouver.

"We must conclude by saying that George Vancouver simply got in over his head with his commander role on the Pacific voyage, and that he could not extricate himself from the resulting issues and consequences.

"Nevertheless, due to his outstanding navigation and mapmaking, his name lives on in this great city and the large island to the west. A large, golden statue of George Vancouver sits atop the British Columbia legislative building in Victoria. He is remembered, even if imperfectly.

"I hope this presentation has been interesting for you; thank you for attending. When you gather tomorrow for the auction of the many items related to this story, perhaps they will seem even more special to you."

Following the presentation, everyone returned to the reception area where food stations had been laid out and the bars were again open.

The initial conversations rehashed the lecture, much as had occurred at the intermission.

Perhaps the most common thought was, "How tragic; what a sad ending for George Vancouver."

45

However, the conversations soon drifted back to the pending auction as dealers and collectors speculated on tomorrow and repeated their many conversations from the previous two months.

Hadrian Wall and Chester Chalk observed the gathered group.

"Well, Stone, there is a good turnout of heavyweights. BB Bookshelf Auctions seems to have organized and scheduled this very well."

"For sure; Professor Robertson did a good job positioning many of the items in the sale. Gunther Schultz must be pleased with that."

"I agree."

"You know, he probably increased my personal interest in some of the ephemera, especially the key illustrations and the letter."

"Then Robertson certainly did his job."

Margaret Thomas chatted with Louis Wing.

"It will be interesting to see how the sales prices compare to the Cushing sale," she commented. "People who missed out there on some of these same items may be more determined now."

"I guess so," he replied, "but, I am really only interested in things that aren't comparable. I bought what I wanted there."

She flinched a bit at that. Was there a hidden message?

Colin Mackenzie was talking with Lord Southley, the British High Commissioner to Canada, and an avid book collector in his own right. He had been working with Colin on bidding tactics.

"I hope we have some success tomorrow," Lord Southley said.

"We will see, my Lord. There is a lot of competition here, but I think you will be competitive and maybe we will surprise some people."

Alan Page stood back from the crowd a bit. His Chinese client was not here, but he would be awaiting a phone report on his success as soon as the auction concluded.

Herb Trawets mingled with the many familiar faces. Chatting with Colin, he simply said, "Well, let's hope inventory values go up again tomorrow."

Colin smiled. "Maybe we will influence that."

46

By ten thirty the next morning people were gathering in the hotel ballroom. Coffee was available. There was a steady hum of conversations in the room.

Again, a podium, display tables and easels, many rows of chairs, and an array of telephones were all in place.

The sale was scheduled to begin at eleven, the same time as the Cushing auction, adjusting for Pacific Standard Time here.

Gunther "Gunfire" Shultz was there to conduct the sale, attesting to its perceived importance. He was assisted by a reputable auctioneer from their Canadian office, as much to soothe local sensitivities as being necessary.

Herb Trawets looked over the crowd as he prepared to sit in the front row.

The room was full. He knew many of the people who were present, and he knew that there were many others connected by phone.

There were also quite a number of interested observers who had no intention of purchasing anything, including Jonathan Robertson

A few reporters were present. They had been mingling with the gathering crowd, asking questions. They were noticeable due to their ever-present notepads.

Herb also noticed two very somber-looking men, dressed in dark suits, sitting in the back row. For some reason, they looked a bit out of place. They seemed to be scanning the crowd quite intensely, often looking down at a sheaf of papers that one of them held in his lap. He wondered if they were government officials, possibly tax collectors or customs agents determined to be sure all the appropriate payments were made. Herb, as with every other book dealer, was always irritated by the elaborate paperwork that was required to document the international buying and selling of old books.

Given the number of items, the sale was expected to take about four hours. However, Gunther had broken it into three sessions, with a coffee break between each part. The first session would handle all of the antiquarian books. The second session would cover the various paintings, maps, and other ephemera from the collection. The last session would only have the Vancouver journals. Gunther had designed it for maximum impact.

Over the first session, which took about two hours, the action was lively, with a balance of dealers and collectors bidding.

If anyone was looking for a trend, it seemed prices aligned very well with the auctioneer's estimates, closely paralleling the Cushing levels. Given the location and the general focus of the collection, perhaps items more directly linked to the George Vancouver saga, such as the journals of Meares, Dixon, Portlock, Broughton, and Menzies or the Spanish journals of Malaspina and Espinosa, attracted slightly higher prices than the journals of the Russians, such as Kotzebue and Lisiansky, or the general voyages of Anson, Dampier, La Perouse, and Wilkes.

Books related to Canadian explorers, such as Alexander Mackenzie and David Thompson, also did well.

After a coffee break, the second session continued the trends of the first in terms of bidding and prices.

First, there were two dozen vintage maps that depicted the unfolding knowledge of the Pacific coast of America from the sixteenth to the eighteenth centuries.

Maps from the mid-1500s by Munster and Rasmusio essentially showed nothing north of Mexico.

By the late 1500s maps by Ortelius showed a northern Pacific coastline that was very exaggerated in its western direction, influenced by voyages such as Francis Drake's, but limited by the fact that, at that time, determining longitude at sea after long voyages was almost impossible.

In the 1600s many maps, such as those by Briggs, Speed, Coronelli, and Sanson, showed California as a large island, either misinterpreting the Mexican Baja peninsula or the result of a deliberate program of disinformation by the British government about Drake's discoveries.

Through the mid-1700s many very speculative maps by Zatta, de l 'Isle, and others showed large inland seas and channels crossing back into the mid-continent, based on fanciful tales of phantom explorers and the desire to find a transcontinental passage.

In the 1750s and 1760s maps by Muller and de Vagaundy appeared that had a reasonable approximation of the location of the coast, based on the voyages of Bering, the Russian explorer.

James Cook's map of the early 1770s accurately displayed the shape and longitudinal position of the Pacific coast of North America for the first time, although it did not have details such as Vancouver Island or the Queen Charlotte Islands.

The maps all generally sold in the predicted range of value.

Finally, George Vancouver's detailed survey and maps provided the full picture of the coast. Individual copies of his maps sold for between $10,000 and $25,000, more than predicted.

Then, the auction moved on to the various illustrations. Prices were firm.

The illustrations depicting the death of Cook in Hawaii by George Carter and John Webber sold for $18,000 and $12,000 respectively.

The rare print depicting the capsizing of the La Perouse survey boat in a storm off the Pacific coast in southern Alaska, by Louis Crepin, sold for a respectable $10,000.

Dodd's illustration, *The Spanish Insult to The British Flag at Nootka Sound*, depicting the capture of Colnett's ship by Martinez, sold for a premium $25,000.

Gilray's newspaper cartoon lampooning George Vancouver, *The Caneing on Conduit Street*, also sold for a premium at the same $25,000.

Hadrian Wall bought both of those previous two items, certainly inspired by the presentation the previous evening.

The last item in this session was the handwritten letter by George Vancouver, written just a few months before his death. Jonathan Robertson had described it in emotional detail during his speech.

The auctioneers had deliberately placed this item here, anticipating that it would be a good preamble to the sale of the Vancouver journals. They hoped that it would generate a premium price from buyers who wanted a Vancouver original item, but who would not be competing for the actual journals.

They were not disappointed. The letter sold for $50,000. Again, Hadrian Wall was the purchaser.

47

The final coffee break was taken.

There was quite a buzz in the room as everyone anticipated the final item, the Vancouver journals.

But when the auction reconvened, the room seemed quieter than it had been in the other sessions—almost as if people were holding their breath.

Louis Wing sat in the front row, slightly off to one side, but in clear view of Gunther Shultz. He was going to bid himself. He had not included Margaret Thomas in his final thoughts; she had nothing to add. He had not contacted Herb Trawets again; he could not think of any reason to do so. By positioning himself in the front, he hoped to send the message that he was serious and that he didn't even need to see who else was bidding behind him. He was poised for action.

Colin Mackenzie sat with Lord Southley, talking in low tones, as if they hadn't discussed their bidding plans extensively before.

Hadrian Wall and Chester Chalk sat together. Chester had a bidding mandate from a Toronto collector but he doubted it would be adequate.

Alan Page sat alone, just looking forward to watching the bidding unfold. He had bought a few items for his Chinese client in the earlier part of the auction, but he had no mandate for the journals.

There were a half-dozen phone stations occupied by auction agents. Potential bidders were on the other end of those lines. One of those was Simon Katz in New York. He had arranged to bid for a collector from Boston, but, as with Chester Chalk, he didn't really believe that his limit would be competitive, which he had candidly told the collector. Thus, he had not travelled to Vancouver.

Jeremy Boucher had similarly not come to Vancouver. He didn't have a legitimate bidder for the journals either. He had bid unsuccessfully on a few of the earlier books.

Vancouver's Vengeance

Herb Trawets again sat in the front row, on the opposite side of the room from Louis Wing. He suppressed a smile as he thought about the surprise he was going to spring.

Gunther Shultz called the session to order. He described the Vancouver journals in detail, emphasizing their uniqueness, of course.

If "Gunfire" had utilized a slow pace for effect a few times before, that was nothing compared to his glacial pace this time. He believed that for very high priced items it was better to give bidders time to think and to consider the consequences of not winning, rather that hoping they would get caught up in a faster bidding frenzy.

Since Gunther had no idea what the ultimate bid was going to be, he did not start with the usual auctioneer trick of asking for an opening bid near the upper end of his expectation. Although that tactic never solicited such an opening bid, it often served to set the tone and expectation for bidders.

He opened by asking for $100,000, a bit under the price that the Cushing set had sold for in the last auction. A few hands were raised and he recognized Chester Chalk. "Now, $125,000?" he continued.

In a paced manner, the bids moved up past $200,000. Since there were a number of interested parties involved, Gunther moved the recognition around: Chester at $100,000; a local dealer at $125,000; the phone agent for Simon at $150,000; a Calgary collector at $175,000; Chester again at $200,000; and the phone agent at $225,000.

After a slightly longer pause, Colin Mackenzie bid $250,000. Chester was finished, as was Simon, who had already used his plus-one bid flexibility.

Then Louis Wing entered the action for the first time. Not raising his arm, but clearly visible to Gunther, he showed three fingers, $300,000. He had not even bothered with the normal next step of $275,000, hoping to send a message of intent, if not intimidation.

Colin responded at $325,000.

Louis bid $350,000; Colin $375,000; Louis $400,000.

Then, again after a long pause, Herb Trawets quietly, but audible to everyone, said, "$450,000."

For a moment there was complete silence, even from Gunther.

Louis could see Herb, who was looking away from the podium and showing no emotion at all. Had the President changed his mind? How serious was the bidding going to get now?

Louis, actually raising his hand this time, said, "$500,000."

Herb: "$550,000."
Louis: "$600,000."
Silence.
Gunther Shultz briefly resumed his auctioneer patter again, but with little energy. Everyone knew that the auction was over.

As the crowd dispersed, a number of people went up to Louis and congratulated him. Herb was one of those.

"Herb, you surprised me a bit," Louis immediately said.

"Well, Louis, when I didn't hear back from you, I went out to find a new collector."

"New?"

"Yes."

"Interesting."

"Congratulations again. Take care."

Herb then continued to mingle, finally meeting up with Colin Mackenzie.

"It was good try, Yrrab. I knew we were likely to get outbid by Louis, but it was a creative idea to attempt to confuse him with your bidding, rather than me continuing. We were at Lord Southley's limit with your last bid."

"Right, Colin. Well, I guess we'll just get on with selling the collection we accumulated last summer."

"Certainly; I'll keep you informed."

As he was walking out of the auction room, Jonathan Robertson turned to a couple of people who had attended his lecture and said, "George Vancouver would have been amazed to know that his journals would someday sell for such a huge price. For him, it would be a bit of vindication, or perhaps even vengeance."

BOOK THREE

The Pursuit

48

Agent Wilson and Inspector Fleming had entered the auction hall just before the sale started that morning. They sat in the back row and observed all of the action. Without saying much to each other during the proceedings, they were both astounded at the amount of money that was bid for old books—tens and hundreds of thousands!

In the period before the auction started, they had wandered through the crowd of participants and listened in on the various conversations. They didn't hear anything of significance, but they did get a sense of the dynamics.

Wilson had a profile of many of the participants to supplement his observations in San Francisco. He frequently glanced at his notes as he scanned the crowd from his back-row observation point. As the auction unfolded, he was able to identify people such as Louis Wing, Herb Trawets, and Colin Mackenzie. He certainly picked out Alan Page very early and watched him constantly.

He sensed that Page was a somewhat secondary player in the business. He had bought a few books, notably ones about Russian explorers.

The auction ended about one thirty in the afternoon. Some people mingled around for a short while afterwards to talk about the results.

Inspector Fleming had kept his eye on Alan Page as he prepared to depart. As agreed with Agent Wilson, they didn't want to draw attention to any contact with Page. Thankfully, Alan started to leave alone after talking briefly to a few other dealers and to Louis Wing.

"Mr. Page, could I talk to you for a minute?" said the Inspector.

"Sure," replied Alan.

"I am Inspector Fleming with the RCMP. I, and a colleague of mine from the FBI, would like to chat with you."

"What's this about?" asked Alan, surprised, and somewhat concerned. He didn't think he had done anything particularly wrong lately.

"We just hope you can help us with an investigation. We would like to keep the conversation confidential, and wonder if you could meet us in an hour, say 3:00 p.m., in the lobby of the Pender Howe Inn, a couple of blocks from here."

"I guess so. But surely you can tell me something more than that."

"Not here. We don't want others to observe us."

"OK, I'll be there," Alan said, understandably betraying a bit of anxiety in his voice.

49

Alan headed to the lounge in the Hotel Vancouver and found a private booth in the corner where he could think about what had just happened.

There were sometimes actions involving international travel and the buying and selling of books that skirted the rules on customs duties and sales taxes. Bookkeeping was complicated. Could it be that? That might explain their presence at the book auction and their need to talk out of sight from other dealers. But that didn't seem quite right. Why would an FBI agent be in Vancouver for that type of thing? Wouldn't that be the IRS or the Treasury? In any case, he hoped he wasn't going to need to go through a painfully detailed audit of his records

Then he thought, "The Chinese; of course. It must have to do with them."

In reality, he didn't know very much about the people he was dealing with. He simply bought books as instructed and received a fee. That would be easy to explain.

He arrived at the Pender Howe Inn right at three and immediately saw Inspector Fleming and another dark-suited man standing off to one side of the lobby.

Inspector Fleming made the introductions.

"Mr. Page, this is Agent Wilson of the FBI."

"Hello, Mr. Page. Thank you for meeting us."

"Right. What is this about?" responded Alan directly. He was anxious.

"I'll explain in a minute," responded Wilson. "We can meet in a small conference room just down the hall. That will give us some privacy."

Then Agent Wilson turned to his companion and said, "Thank you for all of your help, Inspector Fleming. I can take it from here. I'll be in touch."

Obviously Fleming was not going to learn any more details about the FBI investigation; he was not surprised.

"My pleasure; let me know if there is anything else we can do for you before you leave town."

Efrem Wilson and Alan Page walked down the corridor and entered a small meeting room where an urn of coffee and some soft drinks had been laid out.

Wilson had decided that his initial approach to Alan Page would be as non-threatening as possible. He wanted Page to presume he was just being interviewed for information, consistent with the story Ray Cartwright had related.

Of course Alan was a prime suspect. So far, he was the only person actually known to be involved.

"Thanks again for seeing me, Mr. Page. I am investigating a book purchase and I'm hoping that you can help me with some information."

"Fine," Alan replied, still struggling to figure out what was up.

"President Cartwright bought a document a couple of years ago that I understand you facilitated. I want to ask you about that."

Alan swallowed hard. "Oh boy!" he thought. "I didn't predict this."

Wilson continued, "Can you tell me about that deal? Who was the seller, for example?"

After a pause to gather his thoughts, Alan responded.

"As I can explain, Agent Wilson, I didn't know the seller. What's the problem? Was the document stolen? I did wonder where it came from."

Wilson was pleased with that reply. He had obviously caught Page by surprise, and yet, his first reply was quite direct and inquisitive, not evasive or defensive.

"Tell me how the whole transaction occurred, in detail, please."

Alan took a big breath and began.

"It started with a phone call. The caller knew a lot about me, especially that I was somewhat independent, fearless, and knew the Vice-President, at least on a customer basis.

"He described a special document in general terms: Sir Francis Drake, late 1500s, thin quarto-sized in covering boards.

"He said it had been found in an old family home in England. It was being sold privately and secretly. Otherwise, he would need to donate it to some university or the British Museum.

"The asking price was $2.5 million. I would receive a $200,000 commission. The payment would go to a bank account in the Bahamas.

"If Vice President Cartwright was interested, the document would be delivered directly to him. I was not going to touch, or even see it.

"I was given a phone number to contact the caller. He said it was a pre-paid cell phone that couldn't be traced. He also said his name was Frank Drake, obviously a weak attempt at humor."

Agent Wilson followed up on Alan's reply with many questions.

"Why did the seller pick you?"

"I have no idea; reputation, I guess."

"Did you judge the document to be authentic?"

"I couldn't say. I never inspected it. I only had one brief glance at it later, when Vice-President Cartwright was examining it in his office."

"Did you think it was stolen?"

"I had no idea. The seller's story had a slight ring of truth but I realized it might be a cover-up. I had no way to tell."

"What did the seller sound like?"

"At the time I recall thinking he had a bit of an accent, but I couldn`t place it. A combination of American and British? Canadian? But that didn`t seem quite right. I didn't know. He did sound educated and knowledgeable."

"So, you approached the Vice-President, he said yes, and the money flowed?"

"Not exactly. I guess when you`re in political positions such as that your money gets tied up in trusts and such things. There was a delay of a few weeks before the deal was completed."

"Didn't the Vice-President seem skeptical? Concerned about the deal?"

"Yes. However, there were laboratory tests provided. I can't believe that he didn't get some expert advice, even with the request for secrecy."

"How did this Frank Drake pay you?"

"It was just agreed that I would be paid the commission directly by the buyer. The remainder, $2.3 million, was to be transferred to the Bahamas."

"The Vice-President gave you the $200,000?"

"Yes. Actually, I recall it was a certified bank check made out to the bearer."

Agent Wilson continued to be impressed, and surprised, by Alan's candidness and ease of answering. He tended to believe him, but he would do some follow-up investigation.

"Thanks for your time. I will probably be in touch again."

"What is this about? Was it stolen? Did Frank Drake not pay his taxes?"

"I'm afraid I can't tell you any more right now. However, I must ask you to keep this conversation very confidential; we don't want anyone to get wind that we're investigating the transaction."

"Sure."

"Thanks again."

50

Agent Wilson returned to Washington and briefed Director Stephens on his findings.

She decided that a face-to-face meeting with herself, the President, and Agent Wilson was probably a good idea. It was time to get something on the record, even if it was just a meeting-log entry. That would be in the President's best interest, whatever developed.

The next afternoon they met in the President's office.

Agent Wilson summarized his findings.

"Alan Page's story, as improbable as it seems, does hold up. I truly don't think he knows anything else.

"The money that was sent to the Bahamas was widely distributed in a complicated manner. We don't have any other leads there."

Sybil Stephens directly asked the President, "Sir, do you have any concerns that the situation could turn into a personal or political issue for you?"

Ray Cartwright laughed. "Well, obviously, I could be made to look foolish, but I would deserve that. However, the fact that I voluntarily brought this to your attention, and we are pursuing justice, obviates the need for any secrecy or cover-up if it does become public. I'd just have to rely on my 'Ah, shucks' explanation."

The others smiled and nodded their heads.

"OK, I think we're good on that front," said Sybil.

"What do we do next?" asked the President.

"We are at a bit of a dead end, I must admit," replied Agent Wilson. "Are you sure no one else knew about the document?"

"As I told you, I did get some general advice about verifying documents from Jeremy Boucher, even back then, and I did consult with Herb Trawets and Colin Mackenzie about Drake's history. I didn't describe the actual document to them, and they certainly didn't see it. Each of them actually cautioned me about buying anything unproven; they were both quite specific and adamant about that. I don't see anything to follow up there."

"That seems right, and we still want to prevent our interest in the matter getting back to the forger," agreed Agent Wilson.

"I have one far-out idea," Ray said. "I re-read the report that Jeremy Boucher wrote about the document and why he concluded it was a fake.

One of his points was that the document was printed, not handwritten, and he was skeptical that Drake would have done that. Well, it was printed."

"I don't follow," Director Stephens said. "How does that help us?"

"Don't you think that the forger would have made more than one copy? Why go to all that trouble and only make one? Maybe we could flush it out."

"You mean that you would ask for a second one?"

"No, but someone could."

Sybil turned to Wilson, "Let's try to develop some ideas along that line."

With that, they left.

51

Agent Wilson returned to his own office, having been given the mandate by Director Stephens to create a plan.

"I guess we can't just run an ad in the *New York Times* saying we are willing to pay a lot of money for a fake Sir Frances Drake document, and ask the person to drop it off at the FBI office," he had said to the others as he was leaving the White House.

It was obvious that any action needed to involve Alan Page. After all, in the mind of Frank Drake, the forger, Alan was the only person, other than the President, who knew about the existence of the Sir Francis Drake document.

Besides that, Wilson had absolutely no idea how to proceed. Alan was an expert on old books; maybe he would have some ideas.

Wilson flew to Phoenix to meet with Alan, who had returned home from Vancouver.

He reminded himself that Alan Page was not aware that the Drake document was a fake; he believed the investigation involved tax evasion, or perhaps robbery.

He opened the conversation very generally. "Mr. Page, do you have any ideas on how we could track down Frank Drake?"

"Please call me Alan; Mr. Page sounds so formal and it makes me a little uncomfortable."

"Fine, Alan."

"I don't really have any ideas. After I received my payment from Ray Cartwright, I did try to phone Drake one more time, to thank him, and also to indicate I was always available for other assignments. After all, I had made some good money. However, the phone number I had been using didn't connect. I just got a recording that the number was no longer in service. I didn't know what else to do, but it didn't really matter, since Frank Drake knew how to get hold of me if he wanted to."

"If you wanted to try harder, what would you do?"

After thinking about that, Alan said, "Well, I guess I could place an item in a newspaper, or more likely in the magazines dedicated to antiquarian book collecting, saying something like 'Frank Drake, call Alan.'"

Wilson almost laughed; that was essentially what he had joked about with the President and the Director.

"If we did something like that, would you work with us to try to build up a closer connection with Drake?"

"You mean, would I work with the FBI to track Drake down?"

"Yes."

"Is that legal? Can I, a regular citizen, work with the FBI to catch a tax evader?"

"The situation might be a bit more complicated, but it would be legal."

"More complicated? Was the document actually stolen?"

"Maybe."

"Even if I was willing to work with you, what could I say to entice Drake to follow up?"

"We did come up with one concept. I know you didn't see the document that President Cartwright purchased up close, but it was typeset. That means that there is probably more than one copy. Maybe Frank Drake can get another copy."

"You mean, if he stole one, perhaps he can steal another one?"

"Again, maybe. Of course, until we find out who Frank Drake is, we don't know that he stole it."

"Oh, so you don't actually know where the document came from in the first place after all?"

"No. We're just speculating there. There's no previous record of it."

"Stolen from some British family's library? Government archives? The British Museum?"

"Who knows?"

"That also means it could legitimately be out of a family estate."

Wilson's tale was becoming more complicated as he played Alan Page along. However, he saw no reason to disclose the real nature of the document's tainted status. That disclosure might come in handy later.

"I could try to help. But it seems that we will need more of a story to lure Frank Drake into our trap," Alan continued.

Wilson knew then that he had Alan captivated and engaged. Words like lure and trap betrayed excitement; Alan was going to be a junior G-man, every kid's fantasy.

"What else do you suggest?"

"How about if we line up a second buyer ahead of time?"

"Perhaps. Can you suggest someone? Although, the more people who get involved with a scheme, the more difficult it is to keep it confidential."

"If we're looking for someone who can easily spend a few million dollars on a rare document related to historic voyages of exploration, there is no one bigger than Louis Wing in California."

"The electronics tycoon?"

"Yes, he spent millions at the recent auctions in New York and Vancouver. You probably noticed him in Vancouver; he bought the George Vancouver journals."

"He sounds perfect."

"Well, I can hardly call him and say, "How about working with me to buy a rare book that might be stolen, so the FBI can chase down some back taxes?"

"No, I would need to arrange that. Perhaps even use the President." That was a slip-up by Wilson.

"The President? He is personally involved in chasing tax evaders?"

"Not quite. However, it was his concern that the original deal might not be legitimate that brought all of this to our attention," he replied, trying to recoup his cover story.

"Oh."

"Anyway, this has been very helpful. You have had some good ideas. I will go back and try to flesh out a program. I'll be in touch, but be sure to call me if you think of anything else. Thanks."

After Wilson left, Alan Page reviewed what had happened.

"Something's not quite right," he mused. "Why would the President suddenly get concerned about the Drake document being stolen? That was an obvious question years ago, when the deal was done. Now he has brought in the FBI to investigate if he was the purchaser of stolen goods? That seems risky for a politician."

He would just have to wait and see what developed. He was sure glad that he had declared the commission on that original transaction on his income taxes.

52

Wilson returned to Washington and again briefed Director Stephens on what he had learned and the idea that he had developed with Alan Page.

"That idea sure seems like a long shot. There needs to be a second copy, and this fellow, Frank Drake, needs to rise to the bait. Then we need to set a trap that he will fall into," she replied.

"Agreed. But I don't have any other idea."

"We'll only get one shot. If Drake gets any inkling that we are aware of him and his fake document, he will disappear into thin air."

"I know. A lot will depend on Alan Page's credibility. That's one of the reasons I didn't tell him the truth about the document. He still thinks it's related to some combination of stolen goods and tax evasion."

"Do we know much about this Louis Wing?"

"I had the office do a quick scan for information about him while I was flying back from Phoenix. He is a very rich man who made his fortune in telephone electronics. He collects old books. He appears to be quite respectable, and respected. Although he does not seem to be involved in politics at all, he is a quiet, inactive donor to the President's party."

"I would like to keep the President out of this as much as we can. We could approach Wing with a story related to robbery and taxes, as you did with Alan Page. I wouldn't need to mention that it involved the President."

"I suppose so."

"OK. Let's pursue this. Work up a detailed plan, using Alan Page as necessary. As you said, he will be our leading actor. In fact, he will be the only one on stage with a speaking part. Once I have reviewed it, I will arrange to contact Louis Wing. I have the feeling that he might require some coaxing to get involved."

Agent Wilson spent the next few days working on the plan, trying to anticipate what could go wrong, and what contingent actions they could organize.

The biggest downside that he could see wasn't that Frank Drake would avoid their approach; it was that he would walk away with another few million dollars. Obviously his money laundering skills were very good. This time it would be government money at stake; Louis Wing wasn't going to just make a donation.

53

A week later, Sybil Stephens read through Agent Wilson's plan and decided it was worth pursuing, although she knew the odds of success were no more than fifty-fifty. It depended on so many things going right in a linear manner, with few contingent paths.

She briefed the President on the plan, since it was his money that had been lost, and it was his reputation that was being put at risk.

"We'll certainly try to keep you out of the picture, both for your benefit and because everything will fail if Frank Drake gets any indication that the new approach links back to you in any way."

"Alright. Let me know what happens."

Then she arranged a meeting with Louis Wing. It had taken some time to prepare everything. It was now April and he was going to be in New York, again attending the New York Antiquarian Book Fair, among other things.

Her approach to Louis was carefully thought through and well scripted. In reality, they just needed to use Louis Wing as a benign conduit for information and funds.

Louis was quite perplexed as to why the Director of the FBI wanted to meet with him. If anything, he had been more than fastidious about his taxes, regulatory filings, patent licenses, and even border crossings. He knew that technology was becoming elaborate and insidious in processing and cross-checking information. He believed that to avoid being in any government-watch system was far more important than saving a few tax or customs dollars. The hassle of time-wasting investigations, customs delays, and eventual costly lawyers was not worth it. He actually believed that if the IRS conducted a tax audit on him, he would likely get a refund.

He was also not intimidated by government officials. He knew they were determined and dedicated in their roles. He also knew that they tended to work much harder than the public's general perception. By admiring and accepting that, he also knew that he was always on firm ground sticking to the facts of a situation. He always liked the quote to the effect that telling the truth was better than lying, because you didn't have as much difficulty remembering it.

They met in the sitting area of the Director's suite at a midtown hotel. She was far too recognizable to the public and the press to have private meetings in open places.

He had a lawyer from the New York office of the firm he dealt with in San Francisco wait in the lobby. However, entering the suite and seeing that she was alone, which totally surprised him, he knew he would not need the support.

"Mr. Wing, thank you for making time for me."

Louis smiled. As if one could ignore the Director of the FBI.

"I must admit that I'm quite perplexed, but curious, about this meeting." As always, Louis was direct and honest.

"I can understand that. For reasons that will become apparent, I could not give you any advance information. I appreciate that we are meeting alone." Sybil matched him for candidness.

"If you will allow me, she continued, "I would like to tell you about a rather complicated situation where you may be the only person who can help me."

Now totally intrigued, Louis nodded.

"Here is a story of a situation that has played out over a few years.

"An antiquarian book collector was approached to buy a previously unknown document related to Sir Francis Drake's epic voyage. The deal had to be kept absolutely secret. The price was a couple of million dollars.

"The dealings involved a middleman who never met the seller, nor ever saw the document. The purchaser, after some general investigations, made the deal; the payments went to an offshore account. No record of any taxes being paid on the transaction can be found. We would like to flush out the seller; we don't know who he is.

"With your reputation as a collector, if you would act as a decoy for a similar second purchase, we would hope to find that person. There will be many details to fill in, but that's the general situation."

Sybil thought she had done a good job of summarizing the situation and, presumably, catching Louis Wing's attention.

Louis just looked at her with a blank expression while he absorbed what he had just heard. He took his time. Then, quite calmly, he responded. He was definitely not as awestruck, or as intimidated, as Alan Page had been with Agent Wilson.

"I appreciate your candor and your belief that I could personally help with one of your investigations. My first reaction is to wonder why the Director of the FBI would personally travel to ask me to help apprehend a relatively minor tax evader. We both know that in the grand scheme of government finance this is minor.

"A secret rare book, sold by a mysterious, unidentified seller, through a naïve agent, to a buyer with millions to spend. Now you want to chase some taxes.

"Director, it doesn't compute. What's really going on?"

"Quite right, Mr. Wing. There are many more details. But the gist is true. We need your help."

"That was evasive, I must say, Madame Director. The story just doesn't have the significance to justify this level of involvement." Louis was always focused.

He continued, "If I agree to help you chase a tax evader, I will probably lose many opportunities to buy rare books that I would like to have."

Totally surprised by this statement, Sybil just asked, "How so?"

Louis elaborated:

"The world of rare book buying and selling is complicated. It's a truly international business, and many transactions cross many jurisdictions. Imagine a British book dealer who buys a book at a book fair in Australia, displays it at a couple of fairs across the United States, and sells it to a Canadian collector. He ships the book to the Canadian, after returning to his home base in London.

"The book has crossed at least three international borders, has attracted potential duties and sales taxes in even more jurisdictions, and has been fluctuating in value as the currencies of four countries move around. I cannot imagine how the book dealers manage to account for all of that, even with the best of intentions.

"Anyway, I buy books and they deliver them. If they need to work some elaborate accounting and delivery systems, just to stay sane, that's their business. I know it's almost always a matter of debits and credits, not real taxes for them. It all averages out for them, and even for governments I expect. However, on a specific transaction it can get very complicated.

"If I were to get a reputation as an agent for customs and tax collectors, I know the deals would diminish. They don't need the hassle."

Sybil stared back at him. "That's amazingly candid."

"It's the truth. Why don't you tell me more of what's really going on?"

For one of the few times in her career, Sybil Stephens didn't know what to say. After a pause, she said, "I will need to make a phone call. Can I be excused for a couple of minutes?"

"Of course."

When Sybil went into the adjoining room, Louis sat back and speculated, "Who does the Director of the FBI call for directions? God, or maybe the Devil? What is going on?"

Sybil placed a call to the President. That was not a simple procedure. She, the Director of the FBI, was calling the President of the United States. Her cell phone was totally encrypted and secure, but still, the call was routed through many security channels.

"Mr. President, Louis Wing won't participate in our plan without more information. He is pretty sharp, and he immediately saw through the simplicity of our story. Can I tell him more?" Sybil never beat around the bush.

After a pause, Ray Cartwright said, "OK. Dammit, Sybil, we have to apprehend this Frank Drake. Fill Louis in!"

When she hung up, Sybil had three impressions, all of which told her how serious the President was about finding the culprit. First, his emphasis. Second, she had never heard him swear before. Third, he had never called her Sybil before; he always used her title of Director. He was determined.

Returning to the meeting room with Louis Wing, she said, "I have more to share with you."

Louis wondered what he was going to hear next.

"The real issue is not taxes. In fact, the document that was involved in the transaction was a fake. It was totally fraudulent."

Louis waited. He knew there was more. If the Director shouldn't be chasing minor tax evaders, she certainly shouldn't be chasing minor forgers.

"The purchaser was President Cartwright."

Louis hadn't expected that. However, his analytical, rational thought process kicked in.

He thought, "So, the Director of the FBI is chasing a fraud case involving the President of the United States. Why would I want to get involved here? Politics!"

Seeing the look on his face, Sybil immediately knew she had lost Louis's interest. She had overestimated her influence and underestimated his independence. Life in Washington could distort your perspectives on such things. She had to try again.

"Although the President could absorb the financial loss, he is determined to have this case pursued, even though it could hurt his reputation. Justice should be done. Besides, we don't know how big this could be; we only know about the one document. The sophistication of the money laundering that was involved might mean that a very large illegal operation exists."

"I can concede that," Louis replied.

"We need you to help flush the culprit out. Working with Alan Page, the book dealer, we will need to fabricate a convincing story to tempt him. You are the only one with the reputation, the interest in rare books, and the money to be credible."

This time, Louis softened his stand. Sybil had appealed to his loyalty, his ego, and his love of adventure. He could play cops-and-robbers for real.

"Well, tell me more of the details. How would this scheme actually work?"

Sybil explained. "Alan Page was involved in the first deal, somewhat innocently. He will attempt to make contact with the forger, Frank Drake. If that works, he will fish for information about a second copy of the document, which is critical to our plan. If there is a second copy, Alan will propose that he approach you to buy it, as he had done with Ray Cartwright years ago. Then the two of you will need to go through the facade of studying the document and buying it. There will be a number of opportunities to apprehend Drake: as he makes contact with Alan and periodically communicates with him; when the new document is delivered; and, in the last instance, when the money is transferred. Remember, we will know everything that's happening as it occurs, and we will even be able to influence some of the action through your negotiations to make the purchase."

"That's pretty creative."

"Only if he takes the bait and there actually is a second copy."

"I will do it. Let's go catch a bad guy."

They agreed to a path forward. Agent Efrem Wilson would be the coordinator. The Director and the President would not get directly involved any more, but Wilson would keep them informed.

In the next issues of the British magazine, *The Book Collector*, and the American one, *Firsts*, a small insert would appear in the advertisement pages: "Frank Drake, SFD beckons. Call Alan P."

They felt the message was specific enough to catch Frank Drake's attention, although totally meaningless to any casual reader. They hoped Drake actually read those magazines.

Given the printing cycles, they would need to wait at least two months to find out.

54

In California, late June, sitting on his oceanfront patio, Herb Trawets had sorted through his morning mail. Now, he was browsing through the *Firsts* magazine that had just arrived. He checked out the list of articles, deciding which ones he would read in detail first. He then glanced at the advertisement pages. He always liked to check on which dealers were promoting themselves aggressively, a habit he developed when he was in the business.

The small insert immediately caught his attention, causing him to stop breathing for a moment.

"What's that? Wow! What's up? Why now?" were his immediate reactions.

Of course, he could vividly recall the events of a few years ago: creating the document; contacting Alan Page to act as a blind agent; waiting out Ray Cartwright's money-raising scheme; getting involved with Cartwright without losing control of his plan; finally, receiving the money after some creative banking logistics.

"Now, what could Alan Page be up to? Am I even going to respond? What's the risk? What could the value be?"

Herb's mind was reeling. He knew for sure that he would not act precipitously; that wasn't his nature. He had to consider all of his options carefully. He even started to make some lists.

Why would Alan Page want to contact him? Most obviously, to make some more money by arranging another deal of some kind.

Why now? There was no clear answer to that, other than Alan was always a bit of a schemer. Alan was at the Cushing and Vancouver auctions, and he seemed to be active.

Could Alan be acting for someone else? Again there was no obvious answer, but there were some rumors that he had been acting for some Chinese buyers,

Could this be some sort of trap? Of course it could be, but there was no apparent reason why that should be the case. His only involvement with Alan, and with an illegal action, was with the Drake document.

He had talked to President Cartwright about the recent auctions, and he was not interested. His life now left little time for book collecting. How could anything have happened to have him question the Drake document now? That idea would seem to be pure paranoia on Herb's part.

Did he want to make another deal with Alan? Perhaps. He had earned a nice fee from Louis Wing at the Cushing auction, and his book-buying adventure for Colin Mackenzie last summer was profitable, but he could use extra money. From his various ventures and the sale of his business, he was able to set himself up quite comfortably in this house on the California shore. However, he would like to travel more. He could visit all of those places that appeared in the explorers' journals of centuries ago: the South Pacific, Australia, South America, Africa, China, Russia, the Arctic and Antarctic. But he dreamt of doing that in reasonable style at a leisurely pace, which was expensive.

Could he make another deal? Well, he did have two more copies of the forged Drake document.

What harm was there in contacting Alan and finding out what he was up to? He would need to be very careful, but he had done it with Alan before without being found out.

Although it was only noon, Herb poured a glass of California Chardonnay and sipped it slowly as he stared out at the ocean. He knew he would go over all of those questions and answers many times before deciding.

55

Waiting is always difficult, even when you know an answer is coming. If you don't know that, time passes even more slowly.

Agent Wilson and his team waited, not knowing if their message had even reached Frank Drake, let alone whether or not he would reply. The magazines had been out in the market for weeks.

Of course, everyone involved had other activities to handle. The FBI teams worked on many other cases. Alan Page continued his book dealings. Louis Wing, who, in reality, was just on standby until something developed, carried on with his many activities.

They all waited for Frank Drake to contact Alan Page.

Alan had been carefully coached and extensively rehearsed on what he would say if Drake called. He was only going to get one chance to be credible and convincing.

With his permission, the FBI had arranged for all calls to Alan's home and to his cell phone to be recorded. This made Alan somewhat uncomfortable, since his phones were always busy, as worldwide sellers and customers contacted him about possible book deals. That was his life; he was the ultimate book scout. Usually, all of his conversations were very private. That was the nature of his business.

However, he had agreed to allow the monitoring for a while. If they didn't get a response within six weeks, he would cancel the approval. He also obtained a second cell phone so he could at least make outgoing calls to people without the FBI listening in. Its ID number was blocked to anyone on the other end so that it didn't get into anyone's system. Often, when he received a call from a legitimate contact and he was sure it was not Frank Drake, he would make up some excuse about needing to hang up for a minute. Then he would call that person back on his new phone. The FBI didn't totally like that, but they conceded that it was probably OK.

During the first weekend in August, Alan attended a regional antiquarian book and map fair in Palm Springs. It wasn't a big fair, but the local promoters had always worked hard to attract good dealers and, therefore, customers, mostly from Southern California.

How do you get anyone to the desert in August? Food, drinks, and the possibility of finding valuable books from the secondary dealers who attended. For Alan it was just a four-hour drive from Phoenix, and he had found some good books there over the years.

Early Saturday evening, after the first day of the two-day fair, Alan was in his hotel room freshening up for dinner. The hotel room phone rang and he casually picked it up, half anticipating a follow-up call from a dealer he had talked to earlier in the day.

"Hello, Alan. I understand you want to talk to me," a voice said. Unmistakably, it was the somewhat strange accent of Frank Drake.

Alan looked at the two cell phones on the bedside table and grimaced. So much for all that planning!

"Frank?" he asked, trying to collect his thoughts and buy a little time. It was showtime.

"Yes." Then total silence. It was up to Alan to continue.

"I'm so glad you saw my message and called me."

Silence.

"I was hoping we could do another transaction. The last one was good for me, and I could use the money."

Silence.

"Do you have anything else that I could sell for you?"

Alan had been carefully briefed to keep the request very general to start with. Anything more specific could be suspicious.

"I thought you were doing well with the Chinese and Russians."

"I did OK, acting for them at a couple of auctions, but they don't seem to need me on an everyday basis. I had hoped they might be a source of books for selling in America and Europe, but they are only buyers."

Herb had made a direct challenge; Alan had responded well.

"Why did you place that message? What do you specifically want?"

It was the big question, immediate and direct.

"I was hoping that you might have access to other books or documents that I could sell for you on a confidential basis," Alan replied, elaborating on his earlier statements.

There it was; the carefully prepared statement. Everything depended on Frank Drake's response.

The simple statement had many messages. It was open-ended about books and documents; it did not specifically refer to the Drake document. It emphasized that Alan could act in a very confidential manner. It implied that it was all related to Frank's secret source of material. Stolen? Who cares?

Herb listened to Alan's responses. They seemed legitimate.

"Alan, let me think about it. I will be in touch."

"Can I call you? We had a private number last time."

"No."

The line went dead.

Alan, sitting on the edge of the bed in his hotel room, took a deep breath. He had known that he might get the call from Frank Drake at any time, but that call had totally caught him off guard. He hoped he had handled it right; he couldn't think of any obvious flaws. He hadn't expected that a contact conversation would be that short. Would he hear back from Frank?

Agent Wilson had set up a procedure to follow if this happened. Alan had a specific phone number to call, and the on-duty officer at the other end would locate Wilson.

Within minutes, Alan's room phone rang again; it was Wilson.

"What happened?"

Alan related the sequence of events.

"OK, let's go through everything again and see what we learned.

"First, he called you at the hotel, not on your cell phone. Thus, he knew exactly where you were at that moment. Who knew that?"

"No one knew it directly from me; I'm a loner, as you know. Of course, many people would have seen me at the book fair this afternoon. And, I have been coming to this event for a few years."

"That means Frank Drake was close by, perhaps having followed you, or he knows your habits very well.

"Second, you say that he referenced your dealings with the Chinese. Who knows that?"

"No one I know of. I keep all such contacts confidential. I suspect that an astute expert might guess at something like that if they watched my bidding."

"That means that Drake has information about your actions over the past months, even before you placed the advertisement in the magazines. He has been watching you. That could indicate a book industry insider.

"Third, Drake didn't give you any response to your proposal. He didn't give you any way to contact him. That has to have been preplanned; he was just fishing to see what you were up to. He is very thoughtful and careful."

Alan was surprised how much Agent Wilson was able to deduce from so little information.

Wilson continued, "Just to be certain: you are sure it was the same person that you dealt with last time?"

"Yes, his voice is quite distinct."

"Well, obviously we don't have any recording of his voice. Calling you at the hotel room was quite ingenious. We are dealing with a very resourceful individual who is always going to be suspicious."

"What now?"

"Alan, we just need to wait again. It's all up to Drake. However, at least now we know he is aware of your proposal and is thinking about it. I will see if our technical people can trace the source of the call you received, but I suspect that will not lead to anything. He was too cautious."

56

Herb Trawets sorted through what he had heard from Alan Page.

Obviously, Alan was a bit surprised by the call when it came, but he reacted easily and responded directly. There was nothing unusual there; Alan was always quick on his feet.

Alan's proposal—actually it was really just a fishing trip—was credible enough, given their history.

The implication of Alan's initiative was quite clear. He believed that he, Frank Drake, had access to valuable items that needed to be sold secretly. Alan had clearly surmised that the original Drake document was stolen or had at least been surreptitiously slipped out of some collection.

Of course, the only thing that Herb had that would respond to Alan's initiative was a second copy of the Drake document.

The downside of working with Alan again was that he could lose control of the second document and not receive any payment. That was always a risk, but there was no value for the document sitting in storage either.

Everything would depend on his being able to maintain secrecy about his identity. He had successfully done that last time.

Last time he had been the initiator. This time, with Alan starting the process, he needed to be even more cautious.

As before, he had purchased a cheap, prepaid cell phone, actually a few of them. He would not use them often, maybe even just once each. He bought them at a very busy supermarket in Las Vegas; no one would ever remember him. Las Vegas was the perfect place. It was full of people, mostly travellers and strangers. Such phones were bought in droves, all part of the "What happens in Las Vegas stays in Las Vegas" mentality. No sense leaving tracks of a phone all over the place.

Locating Alan had not been difficult, since Herb was in no hurry.

After a few false starts, he had located Alan in Palm Springs. He knew from past conversations that Alan often went to that book fair. Midafternoon during the fair, when he knew Alan would not be in his room, he called hotels near the fair's venue, asking for Alan. On the third try he had confirmation of Alan's registration, although obviously he made no connection with him at that time of day. Then, waiting until an hour after the fair shut down for the day, he called Alan on one of his secure cell phones. It had been relatively easy.

Call again or forget about it? They were really the only two options. The answer seemed easy, once he analyzed it. Go for the money, but go carefully.

57

Alan Page was always on the alert for a call. Where would it come from next? He and Agent Wilson had talked over many possibilities, but they realized, given the circumstances of the first call, that they were not likely to guess right. Just be prepared.

After an elaborate search of phone company records for calls that came into the Palm Springs hotel that evening, the FBI decided that a prepaid cell phone purchased in Las Vegas, calling from the Los Angeles airport, was the source. That phone had never been used before or since.

Alan had asked Wilson if he should have some sort of portable recording device, like a tape recorder with a microphone head, which he could stick on any phone when he got a call.

Wilson thought about that for quite a while and almost agreed. Then he decided otherwise.

"Recorders can be detected with good equipment. We know we're dealing with a very resourceful person. He was able to convince you to secretly approach President Cartwright. He was able to launder millions of dollars internationally that we cannot trace. He called you, out of the blue, in a hotel room from an untraceable phone. He might be capable of monitoring such things.

"If we hear from him again, we must work to develop continuing contact. Once we lose him, for whatever reason, he will be gone forever. However, if we do end up dealing with him on a purchase by Louis Wing, we can create the need for many contacts, to clarify things, to arrange logistics, and to make payment. We will have lots of chances. We can't take any unnecessary risks now."

Almost two weeks after the Palm Springs call, Alan was at home in Phoenix. The doorbell rang and when he got there he saw a FedEx courier with a small package. After signing the receipt, he looked at the box.

Besides the normal routing sheets, there was also a black marker message on the wrapper, "Open Immediately." Sensing it was important, he did just that. Inside, there was a cell phone and a note: "Turn on Immediately, Within One Minute."

Recalling Agent Wilson's admonition to not take chances, he turned on the phone and waited, resisting the temptation to call Wilson. Maybe the phone was bugged; who knew?

Two minutes later, the phone rang.

"Hello, Alan," said Frank Drake.

"Hello, Frank."

Silence on both ends for a moment.

"Alan, tell me more about what you have in mind."

"Frank, it's straightforward. If you have some more books to sell secretly, I will do that. If you have other unique voyage or discovery books, we could approach Ray Cartwright again. If the books relate to something else, I will identify a potential purchaser. I can totally keep you out of the picture, as we did last time."

Again, Alan's pitch had been carefully planned. Keep it general; don't presume. Keep it focused on secrecy. Even suggest going back to Cartwright, meaning there was no problem with the last deal. Mostly, try to elicit some positive response.

"Alan, I understand your reasoning. What if the next item is another copy of the same one we sold to Cartwright?"

Herb's statement was designed to get a reaction, with a subtle hint of more deals in the future by using the word "next."

"Oh."

Pause. Don't hint that this was exactly what they had been hoping for.

"Frank, we would need to find another buyer, of course. Cartwright thinks he has the only copy. We will need another buyer to think the same thing."

Keep coming across as a schemer and a willing partner in subterfuge. No compunctions.

Continuing, "Who could that be? There are lots of rich buyers of exploration documents. Frank, my first reaction would be Louis Wing in California. He has lots of money; he spent millions at the recent auctions. And he has a bit of a reputation as a free thinker and risk taker."

The perfect answer; even Frank Drake would realize that.

"Do you know him?"

"Not well, but I have talked to him at book fairs and even at the Vancouver auction. But if I could attract Vice-President Cartwright's attention last time, I can get Louis Wing's attention. That's what I do."

Honest. Positive. Brash.

"You know the story. Why don't you talk to him?"

Wow. Frank had put it right to him. What to say now?

"OK. Is there anything else? How will we get the document to him? Is the price the same as last time? How do I get back to you?"

"Alan, we can figure out the logistics later. The price is now three million; there has been inflation."

"But last time the price was for a one-time opportunity. Now we know there are at least two copies."

Always negotiate. It's expected and it will set up the need for more contacts.

"The buyer must still believe it is the only copy. Very secret. That's your job."

Keep the pressure on.

"And again, how do I report back?"

"You will need some time to set up a meeting and sell the story. I'll be back in touch with you in a couple of weeks."

Keep control. Don't be in a hurry.

The line went dead.

Alan sat back to catch his breath; he felt like he had been holding it for the whole conversation.

He was pleased. Frank Drake had been engaged, and the scheme was proceeding. He was an FBI agent! Sort of!

Before calling Agent Wilson, he placed the cell phone and its packaging in a large plastic bag and put that in his garage. If there was some kind of bug, that should help. He was thinking like a G-man!

The routine was the same as the last time. He contacted Wilson via his office, and when they were connected he provided a summary of the contact.

Then, again, Wilson dissected the event:

"The phone rang just minutes after it was delivered. That means Drake was monitoring its delivery, probably on the FedEx tracking system. The devices that couriers carry provide instantaneous updates of transactions.

"Alan, as you have described it, you stayed right on script and it does seem to have convinced Drake. Well done.

"There was nothing more you could have done to flush out his location or to get control of future communications. Getting Louis Wing established as the target was critical.

"Our next step is to get the logistics with Louis Wing started. Remember, someone may be watching. As we agreed, you will attempt to contact him through his office. With normal delays, in about ten days you will actually meet in his office.

"Boy, this guy is slick. We need to be alert."

Having returned home from making the call in L.A., Herb took stock.

The call had gone well he thought. Alan's responses seemed genuine. Now, it was a matter of giving Alan time to contact Louis Wing and to test his receptiveness. Louis was the obvious target customer, but, as Herb knew firsthand, he could be independent and unpredictable. Time would tell.

He would wait at least two weeks before contacting Alan again.

58

Alan Page proceeded as planned and met with Louis Wing in his office ten days later. Agent Wilson was plugged into their conversation by telephone.

Wilson summarized the situation.

"You two are having a conversation very similar to the one Alan had with President Cartwright a few years ago. There is a very rare document related to Sir Francis Drake available. Alan has been approached to sell it privately, even though he has not seen the document itself, and doesn't know who the seller is. The seller insists that the buyer keep the transaction secret. The price is three million dollars. Some technical analyses will be provided. If Louis is interested on those terms, the document will be made available for his inspection.

"Louis, you react predictably with skepticism. It makes no sense. It must be a scam. If the document is real, it could be stolen. Why should you trust Alan? Why should you get involved?

"The conversation evolves to why not take a chance? Alan persists: What is there to lose? It could be real.

"Louis, as the conversation unfolds, you become more curious and intrigued. This might be an opportunity to be the sole possessor of a unique document. Why not take a look?"

Alan responded, "That's about what happened last time. I think it's still a credible story to feed back to Frank Drake."

Wilson asked, "Louis, can you think of anything else that Alan should say to Drake?"

"Just emphasize my skepticism. That would be my reaction in any case and, if Drake knows anything about me, he would know that."

"Right. Well, Alan, it's time to wait again. I wonder how he will contact you next. He certainly is creative."

A week later, Alan received a letter in the mail. It was in a plain envelope with no return address, showing a Las Vegas postmark.

The single page note was simple and straightforward:

Alan, I assume you have talked to Louis Wing by now.
I am sure he was initially quite dismissive, perhaps even sarcastic.
Were you able to adequately pique his interest, even if skeptically?

I have no additional information to give you; you have it all.
Should I send the document to him?
Will he accept it on my terms of confidentiality?
Does he agree he will not consult with any dealers? Secrecy is a must.
Does he agree to the price, after inspection and with limited testing?
Simply place a classified ad in the LA Times: FD: (Yes or No) AP.
That's all from me,
Frank

Alan smiled. "So much for stringing out negotiations and having many contacts!"

He called Wilson. They agreed that the only thing they could do was to place the ad with a yes message. They still had no idea who Frank was or how to contact him.

Wilson gave Louis Wing a call to tell him to be on the lookout for a package.

Two days after the ad appeared in the newspaper, a UPS package arrived at Louis Wing's office, marked Urgent and Confidential. It contained a second copy of the Sir Francis Drake testimonial.

Again, Agent Wilson, Louis Wing, and Alan Page had a conversation. This time, they were all on the phone.

Wilson led the discussion.

"From your description, Mr. Wing, we must assume the document is a duplicate of the first one. However, I will have an agent from the local area come to your office to pick it up. We will send it to the lab techs for comparison and to look for any information that might help us."

Alan piped in, a little sarcastically, "Yeah. He has been so sloppy that he probably left his fingerprints all over it."

Ignoring that, Wilson continued, "Now we just put in time again. Remember, he expects you to research the document and to have some laboratory tests done. We will wait for a month."

Louis Wing stepped in. "You know, if this was really happening, I would consult with some expert. I would ignore the admonition to keep it totally quiet; that's my nature. I would show it to Margaret Thomas or Herb Trawets or Jeremy Boucher to get their opinion. I would ask them to keep it secret, which they would for quite a while I'm sure; they know I can be a good source of business."

Alan said, "I know you would. That's why I might not have ever approached you in a real scenario. But, so what?"

Wilson jumped in again, to cut off the gist of the conversation; he didn't want Alan to get any more information. "It doesn't matter. We need to act as if we really want to make a deal. That's the whole premise for making contact with Frank Drake. We need to set up a deal so that we can track him down."

Louis added, "There is a note attached to the document that simply says, 'Have Alan Page insert another ad when you are ready to deal or to return this document to me.' It's unsigned, but obvious in its meaning. Frank Drake is keeping well out of any line of sight. He has outwitted us at every step so far. Remember how we expected to track him down with all of the contacts that Alan would have with him?"

Agent Wilson flinched a bit at that.

59

Agent Wilson again met with Director Stephens to bring her up to date on the latest developments.

"So, in simple summary," she said, "we have made contact with Frank Drake; we have the document; but we still have no idea who he is or where he is."

"That's about it. The next step is to actually make the deal. Tracking the money has to lead us to him."

"Drake has outwitted our plan at every stage so far. Why will we be successful now?"

"Actually, in most cases that involve payoffs, say kidnapping, extortion, or bribery, the instigators almost always control the situation in the early stages. They have the plan and the knowledge; we are always in a reaction mode. We only catch someone in the early stages if they are sloppy or incompetent. Frank Drake is neither of those things.

"He has used one-time, prepaid phones. He has sent parcels by UPS or FedEx that have no traces since he used anonymous street couriers to drop them off. He knows details about Alan Page that many people could determine if they were focussed on that. He routes things through chaotic sites such as Las Vegas or LAX. We don't have any real leads.

"However, when it's time to pay the money, we take control. We have it and there needs to be actual physical contact to transfer it."

"Well, we lost track of the money that was sent by President Cartwright. How do we know that won't happen again?" the Director persisted.

"That transaction happened years ago and we only tried to trace it recently. Once we know where the money is to be sent, we will have our agents work with the receiving bank to ensure it does not get passed on without our contacting the next destinations as well. No money will be sent anywhere that we do not control."

"OK. Go ahead. We need to keep pursuing this. Every time that Drake makes another smart, complex move, the more I think there is a much larger operation behind this—counterfeiting, money laundering, tax evasion, who knows what?"

It was early October when a small insert appeared in the *Los Angeles Times*: "Frank: OK, let's deal. AP."

60

The Seattle Antiquarian Book Fair is held every October. It attracts a wide range of dealers from around the world. Although it is not as exclusive as the California and New York fairs, it is well respected and well attended.

It is a two-day weekend event, with a kick-off dinner on the Friday evening. A guest speaker highlights that evening.

This year the guest of honor was the President of the United States, Ray Cartwright. Being a Seattle resident and avid collector of antiquarian books, he was a natural choice. As the next election cycle loomed, the President was inevitably making speeches at such events. It was a natural fit.

Book dealers, book collectors, as well as politically-connected locals filled the convention center main hall. They mingled freely in the cocktail hour before the dinner.

Hadrian Wall and Chester Chalk chatted in a corner. Hadrian usually attended this book fair, as it was just a one-hour seaplane flight from the harbor in Vancouver to central Seattle. Naturally, he attended the dinner.

"Well, Chester, it will be good to see the President and hear him talk about history rather than current politics."

"Yes, but it is all politics. Just being here makes the point with this audience."

"I wonder what we might find at the book fair tomorrow. The last year has been such a whirlwind of activity with all of the significant books at the Cushing and Vancouver auctions."

"It will be quieter, of course, but something new always turns up if you look diligently enough."

Herb Trawets was there; after all, Seattle had been his home base for decades and he knew most of the people in the room.

He talked briefly with other dealers such as Simon Katz and Jeremy Boucher. Their conversations were very general, mostly about the book fair. He spotted Alan Page in the crowd but managed to avoid him.

Just before dinner was called, he chatted with Margaret Thomas.

"Isn't it great to have the President talk this evening? Herb, you know him better than any of the rest of us; what do you think he will say?"

"Oh, I expect it will be very general. This is a home game for him; he doesn't need to seek many political converts here."

"Well, it's good for our business to have someone so important linked to antiquarian book collecting. Maybe he will make some customer converts for us."

"It certainly can't do any harm."

"I think it's great that Louis Wing is making the introduction of the President. You know that I work with Louis a lot. He credits the President as being the one who introduced him to the idea of collecting antique books, years ago."

Herb hadn't known that. He wondered if that had any significance for him.

After dinner, Louis Wing rose to introduce President Cartwright. Of course, he started by saying that no introduction was necessary, and then he went on to laud the President's leadership and accomplishments. He finished by noting the President's love of history and his avid collecting of books related to the exploration of the Pacific Northwest.

Ray Cartwright's speech was quite non-political, in keeping with the nature of the gathering. He focused on the grand traditions of the area and his admiration for all of the explorers who had first travelled here, whether by sea or overland.

His concluding comment was, "All of us today can look back on the achievements of those early explorers as an inspiration for what we can achieve in the future. With fairly primitive vessels and limited technology, they opened up this region. We salute them all, from Francis Drake to James Cook; from Robert Gray to George Vancouver; from Meriwether Lewis and William Clark to David Thompson."

Herb noted two details in that concluding statement. The President had mentioned the relatively obscure Robert Gray in his list, thus ensuring that an American was included in the maritime attributions. He had also mentioned Francis Drake, although few people associated Drake with the Pacific Northwest.

Agent Wilson was seated at a nearby table, looking over the crowd. He had checked the attendance list and, of course, did not find anyone named Frank Drake on it. Yet, he just felt that Drake was present. Drake's knowledge and actions all indicated he was an insider of this crowd. The problem was that there were over five hundred people present; they were all potential suspects. That's why he had come.

There was general mingling of the crowd after the speech was over. Many people approached President Cartwright to shake his hand and thank him for the presentation. After all, it's not every day that you can chat with the President of the United States. Of course, most of them had someone snap a photo of their contact, often with their cell phones, which usually had the high-resolution technology that Louis Wing had created.

61

Herb, alone now in his hotel room after the dinner had concluded, pondered his next step. It was decision time. What should he do? Take the final step with Alan Page, or just back away and forget it?

Going forward, he would arrange for a money transfer process similar to what he had done last time. The beauty of that system was that if anyone tried to trace the funds, they would just disappear into many small parts; nothing would flow back to him.

His cousin, Nored Trawets, described himself as a money forwarder. He was Persian by heritage, as was Herb, or more accurately, Yrrab.

Nored's father, Remral, who was Herb's father's brother, had moved to America about the same time that Herb's father, Enaed, had moved to Britain. Uncle Remral had developed a money exchange network for his ethnic community. Enaed, on the other hand, had worked in the traditional business of importing Persian rugs after he also moved to America. Herb credited his mother, Tapenna, for stimulating his interest in books; she was an educator and avid reader.

Building on his father's experience, Nored had developed a vast network for money transfers. There were untold thousands of people in the United States who constantly wanted to send money to family members in other countries. They were usually first or second generation immigrants from countries in Southeast Asia, South America, Africa, Eastern Europe, and the Middle East. They could not easily use normal banking channels, primarily because the recipients in those other countries did not have ready access to banks. Nored provided that service.

An added advantage of Nored's network was that he did not always need to physically move the money between countries. He had partners in every region who had money available to distribute to the foreign recipients. They, in turn, wanted to have some of their money safely invested in other jurisdictions, often America. For a fee, Nored could do that for them with the funds he received from the people sending the money to their families. Thus, much of the money collected in the States stayed in the States.

Nored had accommodated Herb, using his network. The money sent to Herb's account in the Bahamas was simply passed on to Nored's regional networks; then on to local distributers; and finally, to many families in many countries. Nored gave Herb offsetting funds, less a fifteen percent commission, of course, right here at home.

Herb had carefully created additional purchase and sale records for his book-selling business to partially explain the money he used to buy his new home. That was not difficult and had little risk of detection, particularly as it was all mixed in with his sell-off of his base business, Herb's Books.

Of course, he paid the necessary taxes. Some of the extra funds had been converted into gold coins which he stowed away. South African Krugerrands and Canadian Maple Leaf gold coins were easily obtained and very easily re-sold to coin dealers when money was needed.

Now, to finalize the Drake transaction, Herb just needed to contact Alan Page one more time.

62

The next afternoon, the opening day of the Seattle book fair, Alan Page was wandering among the various dealers' booths when he heard an announcement over the public address system.

"Would Mr. Alan Page please pick up a delivery at the front reception desk? Mr. Alan Page, please."

Alan immediately knew it was going to be a message from Frank Drake. It fit the pattern of the previous contacts.

At the reception desk there was a simple white envelope waiting for him, with only his name written on the front.

Taking it aside to a quiet corner, he opened it. On a plain piece of paper was written a bank account routing number; nothing more.

Using his cell phone, he contacted Agent Wilson, who was still in Seattle.

They agreed to meet back at Alan's hotel room in thirty minutes. They couldn't meet in public; Frank Drake might be watching.

Wilson looked at the paper.

"Well, that's interesting! It's a U.S. bank account, not a foreign one. Very strange."

He picked up the phone and called the FBI office. He gave them the information and asked them to quickly determine whose account it was.

It didn't take long. Ten minutes later, the phone rang and he was given a short message.

He turned to Alan.

"It's the bank account for the American Prostate Cancer Society. Frank Drake is gone; we've lost him."

"I don't get it," said Alan. "Why would he let us keep the document and have all that money go to charity?"

"Perhaps Drake became spooked by something, and he just bailed out. Or perhaps he has a history of prostate cancer, and that's a priority for him."

"Either way, Louis Wing has the rare document and the money is going to a great cause. I'm sorry you didn't catch your tax evader this time."

"Well, Alan, it's not quite that simple. The Sir Francis Drake documents are fakes, total forgeries. They have no value."

63

Wilson returned to his own hotel room and called Director Stephens.

"We have lost Drake. He sent Alan Page a bank account routing number; it's for the American Prostate Cancer Society. There would be nothing to trace or follow up, even if money was sent."

"He has eluded us, to be sure. However, I don't want to give up on this. The extent of the money laundering procedures and avoided taxes indicates a sophisticated operation," replied Sybil Stephens.

"What do you want me to do?"

"Set up a small task force. Go back through everything. We know there are two copies of that Drake document; maybe there are others. Maybe Cartwright wasn't even the first victim. The prostate cancer link may give us a connection. There has to be something."

"OK, I'll do that," Wilson said. "What will we tell President Cartwright and Louis Wing?"

"I'll call them both. I'll just explain what happened and that we are carrying on with the investigation.

Director Stephens called the President. After hearing about the situation, he simply said, "Good luck, although I think we have lost him. He was too cautious and too smart. Maybe someday, after I retire, I'll write a novel about greed and stupidity combining to trick the hero."

She also called Louis Wing.

"Thanks for letting me know what happened. In reality, I didn't do anything except let you use my name."

"We do appreciate that you got involved."

"You know, quite coincidentally, I am planning to make a donation for prostate cancer research. It is present in my family; my father had it. Most people don't know that it is such a major cause of death for men. There is a saying that men will either die from prostate cancer or with prostate cancer; it's that prevalent."

"That's good that you will support such research."

"I was just thinking, perhaps mischievously, that if I make a public donation, Drake will think it's related to his document. It might give him some reason to believe our deal was legitimate. Maybe that will make him less suspicious or cautious if you get another chance to deal with him."

64

Herb Trawets looked out at the ocean from his patio. Over two months had passed since the Seattle book fair; it was almost Christmas.

He had carefully monitored the American Prostate Cancer Society news sites over that time. Then yesterday there was the announcement of a $2.7 million donation from Louis Wing.

He was sure that Louis had made the donation in response to Herb's note to Alan Page. The amount was exactly right—three million dollars less 10 percent for Alan.

That meant that Louis had not discovered that the Drake document was a forgery. Herb knew that the document would not stand up to close scrutiny by an expert. Apparently Louis had followed instructions, as had Ray Cartwright. He was quite surprised. Louis Wing had seen the extensive confirming information that had been provided with the Vancouver journals he bought at the auction last year; his Drake document had no such pedigree.

However, Herb had bailed out of the deal on the suspicion that something was not right. He certainly wasn't going to have money sent into his cousin Nored's system with any chance of it being tainted. He didn't know any other way to get funds back to himself trace-free.

On the Friday evening in Seattle, right after the dinner, he had been inclined to go ahead with Alan Page and Louis Wing. However, when he woke up Saturday morning, he changed his mind.

He couldn't quite explain it, but seeing Ray Cartwright and Louis Wing together and hearing about their connection had made him nervous.

Also, after the President's speech, people had lined up to congratulate him, actually forming a line to greet both Louis and Ray, shaking hands with each in turn. Herb had been one of the first through and, after that, had watched the others in the room proceed. After Alan Page had greeted Louis and was moving on to Ray, Louis had looked over to Ray and their eyes locked briefly. That had not happened with anyone else. It seemed to send a message.

His instincts had served him well over the years, and he had let them rule this decision. Avoiding risk was more important than securing more money.

Now, he couldn't help wondering if he had made a mistake. He rationalized that the funds going to prostate cancer research was a good thing. He hadn't had the disease, but he knew many men who had.

Still, he could have used the money. On the other hand, if it had all been some kind of sting operation, he was sure that he was safe. His precautions in dealing with Alan should protect him.

He even smiled, thinking that, if it was a trap, the authorities would waste a lot of time and effort uselessly trying to trace the phone calls, delivery services, and other diversions he had used.

Finally, with a shrug, he said to himself, "Well, I do have one more copy left. Maybe someday; who knows? I wonder who else would be interested."

"No, if I didn't follow through this time, it's probably better just left alone."

Epilogue

Epilogue

It was February and Herb Trawets was just finishing his midmorning coffee. He was thinking about the imminent California Antiquarian Book Fair, being held in nearby Los Angeles this year.

The doorbell rang. Opening the door, he saw a fortyish man dressed in a business suit with a white shirt and necktie, somewhat of an anomaly in his relatively casual retirement neighborhood.

"Mr. Trawets?" he asked.

"Yes."

"I'm Agent Wilson with the FBI. May I come in?"

"Certainly."

After they were seated in Herb's living room, he asked, "What is this concerning?"

"Well, Mr. Trawets, it's a bit complicated, but I am investigating the forgery of antiquarian documents and I need some help."

"How did you find me?" Herb asked, with an unintended double meaning.

"I know that you have dealt extensively with President Cartwright regarding his collection of rare books. My investigation is at a bit of a dead end and he recommended you as someone who is very knowledgeable and discreet, and who might be able to give me some new ideas."

"Well, I would be pleased to help you in any way that I can. Tell me more."

The End

AUTHOR'S NOTES AND ACKNOWLEDGEMENTS

This novel is a continuation of the story in my earlier *Drake's Dilemma* and, as then, is a product of my imagination. All errors of fact, language, or style are mine. I have generally used modern American spelling, although there are a few obvious places where British or Canadian spelling was required.

I am a collector of antiquarian books and maps related to the exploration of the northern and western reaches of North America and I am an avid reader of that history. I am fortunate to have copies of many of the publications and maps referred to in this book in my own collection, which provided much of the research information for the story.

I enjoyed sharing my passion about the world of ancient explorers and their amazing journals and illustrations. When I read one of the books in my collection, I don't just think about the explorer's world-expanding adventures; I also realize that the actual book pages I am looking at were read initially by someone hundreds of years ago, perhaps in a London drawing room or Parisian parlor, seeing the other side of the world in words and drawings for the first time! That's very exciting.

Most of my books don't have the special attributes or provenance attributed to the ones in this novel, characteristics which create much of a book's market value. When writing a book that contains prices for many items, I realize that those values can quickly become dated. I have used relatively aggressive valuations for 2013. Ten years ago the values would have been much less; ten years in the future, who knows?

My first novel described the adventures and exploits of Sir Francis Drake in the late 1500s. This book moves the historical references two hundred years ahead to the 1700s, to the time of extensive exploration of the North Pacific by James Cook, George Vancouver, and many others.

In particular, this novel includes an abbreviated description of the voyages, adventures, trials, and tribulations of Captain George Vancouver. I have endeavored to keep faith with the historical record, but there are necessarily some simplifications. I have relied on a number of references for that information, most notably the well-written and very readable biography of Vancouver by Stephen Bown, *Madness, Betrayal and the Lash* (2008). The four-volume Hakluyt Society review of *The Voyage of George Vancouver*, edited by W. Kaye Lamb (1984), has an amazing amount of background information and analysis. I also referenced George Vancouver biographies by George Godwin (1930), Bern Anderson (1960), and E.C. Coleman (2000).

The main storyline again occurs in the modern world of antiquarian book collecting. As before, I ask the experts to accept my generalities. There are many outstanding people in the antiquarian books world who have guided my learning and the assimilation of my collection over the past years. They certainly include Cameron Treleaven, Donald Heald, Jeremy Markowitz, Bjarne Tokerud, Bob Gaba, Eric Waschke, Bernie Lauser, Richard Murian, Mike Riley, Sam Hessel, Helen Kahn, Courtland Benson, Liam McGahern, and many others whom I have met at various antiquarian book fairs or visited in their bookstores. As before, I assure them that all of my characters are imaginary. I know some of them don't believe that!

My wife, Pat, was the encouraging force that gave me the energy to write this second novel. She was the primary story advisor during early drafts and copyeditor and proofreader during the latter stages. I thank her so very much.

Other friends and family members have also provided editorial comments, story line advice, and encouragement. I thank them all, and in particular, my sons, Deron and Deane, who suggested some creative modifications to the story.

Final-copy error spotting and story-tweaking ideas came from many others, including Heather Topolnitsky, Bob Gaba, Murray and Heather Stewart, Carol and Rae Campbell, and Cam Treleaven.

Enjoy,

Barry Deane Stewart, or should that be

Yrrab Enaed Trawets

Vancouver's Vengeance

P.S. Of course Herb was going to elude detection and capture!

The only one who I know of that spotted that simple anagram in *Drake's Dilemma* was my son Deron Stewart (or should I have said Nored Trawets), who, as I said, also provided much valuable input for this book.

I have also noted the great help I received from my wife, Pat(ricia) Anne (Tapenna), and my other son, Larmer Deane (Remral Enaed).

Thanks all.

If you would like to buy another copy of this book, you can contact Trafford Publishing via their bookstore at www.trafford.com or by phone at 1-888-232-4444. It is also available through major commercial websites such as Amazon, Chapters, or Barnes and Noble. Your local bookseller can certainly order it for you.

If you wish to pursue special events, sales promotions, author's participation, or volume purchases, please contact the author at bstewart@ barizco.com

Barry Stewart is a collector of antiquarian books and maps and avid reader of history related to the early exploration of northwest America and the Arctic. He divides his time between Alberta, British Columbia, and Arizona.

He has previously published *Across the Land . . . a Canadian journey of discovery*, which describes Canada's people, places, history, and idiosyncrasies, and *Drake's Dilemma*, the prequel to *Vancouver's Vengeance*.